Milk, bile and **honey**

Nomzamo Dube

ISBN: 978-0-620-88506-5
e-ISBN: 978-1-77605-661-3

Edited by Book Connection Editors
Cover design by Zesh Creatives
Proofreading by Noel Neville Nyathi
Layout & Typesetting by Janet Von Kleist

Published by Kwarts Publishers
www.kwartspublishers.co.za

DEDICATION

Mom and Dad, *ndoboka kwazo.*

Thousands of Africans have been forced by civil wars and or emigrated from their countries in search for greener pastures from other countries and they all have stories to tell. You have not heard them all if you have not read 'Milk, bile and honey'. The story will take you through all sorts of emotions. You will not miss the humour that goes with the story. You will shed both tears of pain and laughter. A good and fluid story telling from Nomzamo. Very well presented.

Ntombezinhle. T. Ngidi

Multi-thematic, dramatically captivating and oozing with wisdom; the bitter experiences throughout the life of a freedom-fighter are sweetened by a love story. Through his eyes, we visualize how the sweet victories of the liberation struggle in Africa ushered in seasons of bitterness, betrayal, cruelty and the strife of civil war. Behind the curtain are two strong women, whose love empowered him to conquer the struggles he faced throughout his life. The story has a beautiful theme that inspires men to make ends meet to sustain their families, and the overarching lesson in the last paragraph of the book; that self-sufficiency and entrepreneurship have the ability to overcome a lot of bitter experiences that we face in life.

Noel Neville Nyathi

Author of Time, Just as She is! & Transformed thoughts; a tale of LITTLE giants

Contents

INTRODUCTION

The birth of a child is not only an elongation of a family; it is a cause for celebrations, jubilations and ululations. Birthing a child is a miraculous and subtle process. A lot could go wrong. A life could be brought to life, yet the carrier of life herself could abscond life in the process or the life brought to life may not make it to life, arriving already asleep. It is a multitudinous situation. The thin line between life and death lies at birth. In spite of the difficult odds accompanied by childbirth, the moment a child escapes the womb, the warmth felt by the carrier of life is unexplainable, it is as if there never was a near death experience. The aftermath of this miracle is itself miraculous.

It was September 30, 1959 when a life was brought to life. In those days, before the midwives could cut the umbilical cord connecting the carrier to life itself, and before life could announce its arrival and aliveness, midwives were quick to check what lay in between the child's legs. Yes, gender mattered. Gender was very important. Boys were celebrated more as they carried the name of the clan for generations and generations to come. Their physical strength also meant more source of food for families as they were agrarian societies, relying on sweat to survive. Girls were regarded as second-class citizens, they were celebrated only as a consolation prize in the hope that they would one day get married and be traded for a number of cattle and goats. Other than being a probable form of wealth, nothing was worth celebrating upon the birth of a girl child.

Ululululu lilililili halalala! It was a bouncing baby boy! Ululations filled the hut, the homestead and eventually the village. Greatness was born. It was akin to the biblical births of Abraham, Isaac and the Messiah himself. Gifts were received left, right and centre. They came in the form of old baby clothes, goats and chicken. This is what people could afford at the time.

The child was born to a 15 year old teenage mother who was herself a school going child. She probably did not understand issues of sexual relations. The topic was taboo in those days; there were no parent-child talks about sex. Girls were only taught to hold their legs together while sitting demurely or tuck their skirts in between their legs as they sat down and to stay away from boys. The reasons for doing so were never disclosed.

Girls were taught that boys were their enemies and this fear conditioning was done at a tender age. Girls grew up running away from their enemies. Boys on the other hand grew up preying on girls. Girls were harmless hare in the lion's den. All boys were fascinated about, was chasing and touching girls. They bet amongst themselves about the number of girls each boy would get. Equality was taboo, no one could let their minds wonder along such thoughts. Boys were never taught that they were equals with girls. The sense of manhood to them was an ordination to a lifetime of privilege awarded to them at birth.

Boys were born already miles ahead of girls in every aspect of life and by virtue of being male species; they were born more equal than girls. George Orwell in his book *Animal farm* elucidated this inequality construct. He explained the metaphoric inequality amongst animals in *Manor farm* when pigs (characters in the sequel controlling the farm government) changed the rules of the farm and the seventh rule, which formerly read, *"All animals are equal"*, was altered to read, *"All animals are equal, but some are more equal than others"*. Thus, although human beings and any living things are somewhat equal in their respective classifications, some have an advanced status of equality than others (men/women, pigs/sheep, horses/donkeys).

Like most children born out of wedlock, the child was born fathered yet fatherless. In the African culture, when a girl falls pregnant out of wedlock, she informs her aunts who have the burden of informing the girl's parents. This is a burden because the aunts may as well be bashed and receive the rage of the parents, particularly the father. They would also be concurrently blamed for not moulding the girl properly to avoid pregnancy or any relationship with boys. Women were inherently guilty even for the misfortunes of others or situations they had no control of.

After informing the girl's parents, they (the parents) would get furious or at least pretend to be furious out of societal expectations. This was regarded as traditional resistance by parents that would soon pass upon the birth of a child.

The girl was called into a family gathering for questioning about who had done the scathing act of impregnating her. She was spitted on by her family for giving away the forbidden fruit, as her virginity was a value addition to her bride price. This pregnancy therefore translated to a reduced *lobola* (bride price) if any. Chastity was everything for girls in those days. Oops! not for girls but for their parents and eventually their husbands. By the way 'men' prefer marrying virgins when they finally decide to settle down after series of hits and run. They are born with a default privilege. Remember!

A family representative was sent to the boy's family (the alleged father), who was a grandson of a chief. He belonged to the royal family of the region. A royal boy could not impregnate a 'nobody', let alone out of wedlock, it was unheard of, and taboo. At least impregnating someone more distinguished would have been more understandable. The child therefore became fatherless even before birth. He was to face life head-on, and alone.

Instead of curling up in a heap of despair, the boy had to man up at a tender age. He grew up with a heart surrounded by a brick and mortar, coupled with anger issues and a boiling temper. His fatherlessness also left him with a void as he had present yet absent siblings. Their relationship would forever be accompanied with mixed emotions and an unconcealable disdain. He felt deprived of his privilege of having a bond with his father and the siblings either saw him as a threat to their father's inheritance or were simply unsure if he was their blood. Whether they were his siblings or not, remained an area of speculation, only his parents could either truthfully confirm or deny; but they chose not to talk about it. In fact, the matter was buried until a time when it refused to be concealed.

CHAPTER 1

Death stalks the living

How could a mother carry a child for nine months and not in the process think about a list of names to pick from? Seemingly, there was unequivocally no hurry in naming a child when I was born. Perhaps there were many explanations to this; the child being unplanned, being born out of wedlock or people were supposedly too busy in their daily routines to think about it. It was during the field-clearing and scorching hot spring season. Every household had to prepare for the farming season, take care of livestock and run their daily errands such as fetching water and gathering firewood.

The spring season is apparently one of the hottest seasons in Southern Africa, a season of the dry heat that precedes the rainy season. Men, women, boys and girls woke up very early in the morning around 4am to engage in their daily chores. The idea was to avoid facing the sun head-on at all cost, hence most duties were done before cocks could crow. Male figures cleared the fields while some gathered livestock and drove them to dams for water. Although cows, donkeys and goats could find water for themselves, each herd had to be closely monitored as livestock would frequently get stuck in muddy dams with low water levels.

Human beings, livestock and wild animals shared the same water source during dry seasons when rivers had dried up. One must diagram the kind of situational co-existence forced by circumstances. Wild animals and livestock that could not escape the mud, died in there mercilessly. Children who notoriously went fishing would in some cases slide into the dam and die before help could arrive. Those dams were a juxtaposition of both life and death.

Women and girls woke up to fetch water from dams before animals could unsettle the water and make it muddy-brown. Others would do laundry while others gathered firewood. School-going children were not excluded from these roles; they would engage in chores and routinely go to school around 7am. Everyone had a role to play in each household.

Perhaps for these reasons, everyone was too busy to think of a name that the newly born was to be given. In Southern Rhodesia, present day Zimbabwe, children's names were not really deeply thought of, their significance didn't really matter, anything historically momentous or trendy could become a child's name. Children could easily be given names of natural disasters such as tropical cyclones or any English word that came to mind or fascinated one (Happiness, Future, Few, Laughter, Engagement, Evidence, War). Names could be anything unusual or even meaningless. As a boy child, my clan name (Kumbudzi) was used as the interim name.

Born with skin the colour of dark chocolate, I was already roasted by the sun in my mother's womb. The kind of skin I had made me invisible at dawn. Extreme conditions seemingly do not discriminate the unborn. Children learn to adapt even before they arrive. My extreme melanin landed me the name "Black". Being born at a time when the South African recording group Ladysmith Black Mambazo was formed, further congealed my name. The group was the talk of the town then, its traditional musical influence overlapped borders. So, other than the name symbolising the cocoa colour of my skin, it was also a celebration of the Ladysmith Black Mambazo group. Eventually my nick and middle name became Mambazo while my school name officially became Black Dube.

After giving birth, mother had to find ways to eke out a living to support herself and her child. It didn't matter anymore that she was 15 years old, she had proven her adulthood to the world. As a result, I never really enjoyed mother's breast milk for long, as any child should. She left home in search for green pastures before I could even crawl. My grandmother (*Gogo*) had no choice but to take over the motherly responsibilities including the lactation role. Yes, I suckled from Gogo until her sagging breasts could produce milk again. This was a normal act in those days.

Breastfeeding is a mystery. The more a child suckles from another woman's breast, the more her body prepares itself to produce milk. Thus, grandmothers breast-fed their grand-children and it was something not out of the ordinary. There weren't any sicknesses such as HIV/AIDS that children could contract through breastfeeding in those days. If there were there, they were very rare. Artificial milk was too pricy for a Black family then.

As we grew up with other boys, we experimented this phenomenon with goats and cows. If a breastfeeding cow or goat died or was at the brink of dying or fell sick, we would identify another to take over the lactation role. At first, both the cow/goat and the calf/kid would resist the strange act. We would pin down the cow/goat at several intervals and force the calf/kid to lactate until they both got used to it and developed the mother-child bond. In most instances, the calf/kid would eventually forget its biological mother. I suppose this is what happened with me. Gogo eventually became my mother. I related well with her more than I could relate with my own mother. Ever since mother left me for the first time, we never got to be in one space for a time as long as one month. Although we visited each other whenever we could, the visits were always short-lived.

I therefore grew up *ko Malume* (my mother's people) and it was shameful at that time. It was synonymous to being an illegitimate child. I was called by names, e.g. *lo ongela yise* (Ndebele)/ *woyu usina tatayi* (Kalanga) loosely translating to "he who is without a father". We lived in Masendu village in Plumtree, a multilingual community speaking predominantly Kalanga and Ndebele sometimes.

Our homestead comprised of an extended family residing in one homestead, although separated by different homes within it. Those homes had no distinct boundary/fence; everyone knew whose hut each belonged to. Each home within the bigger homestead had a separate kitchen-hut and several other huts serving different purposes such as bedrooms, living rooms or storage rooms. Gogo was a widowed woman, the eldest person in the homestead. Her three boy children got married and brought their wives into the homestead. As soon as they married, they extended the homestead and built their huts within the bigger homestead to form a tightly knit extended family.

We shared one huge kraal of cattle; we would slaughter a cow for meat anytime of the year and milked our cows all year round. We depended on animal husbandry and farming for survival. Whenever we sold a cow, we could at least afford to buy bread and other basics like sugar and salt.

Every time a son decided to marry, he was given a number of cattle as a blessing and a start to his marriage. Thus, although there was one herd of cattle and one kraal, everyone knew their own cattle within the bigger herd. Milking was done communally and the milk was shared amongst different homes. So was cattle herding. I enjoyed this communal lifestyle as I had a lot of cousins to play with, day and night.

However, competition and rivalry were inevitable amongst brothers (my uncles) and their wives and they eventually escalated to children.

In any family, there is one member who has a better job than others or is more well up, and hence he/she automatically assumes an elevated status in the family, no matter his/her age. My eldest uncle (Gogo's first born) worked for a big company in the city, hence he was constantly accused of bewitching others so that he and his little family could stay afloat. Whenever misfortune stroke one of the brothers, their family or any of their possessions like the unexplainable death of cattle, blame would be smeared on the rich brother.

Although the brothers had a huge sense of fraternity and on many occasions refused to be unglued, their wives pushed their individualistic agendas. This seems to be common for many married women living with their extended families. Women naturally despise and resent being part of a larger family circle. They desire independence from the influence of their in-laws and prefer nuclear families to extended ones.

Women love their own space and crave for total control over their own affairs. They resent the entanglements of an extended family and in-laws interfering in their relationships or marriages and feeling like a child under someone else's control or under the husband's shared authority with his brothers and parents.

A woman has to pretend like she is content under the government of three brothers for example. In such scenarios, privacy is a struggle. Most women just tolerate their in-laws in order to save their marriages. Husbands on the other hand often think that women are overly dramatic. They fail to understand why their wives cannot try harder to accommodate their larger families and their flaws. For husbands, life is perfect with all their loved ones in one homestead. It is even harder for women whose husbands are easily influenced by their extended family members.

Although we appeared as a close-knit family from outside, we were so divided. Adults would in many instances, pretend to care for each other but tension would be so palpable that it would even felt by children. My cousins were privileged to live with both their parents under one roof. I was the only child without a present mother and father, I depended on uncles to take care of me (buying clothes and paying my school fees). What I resented the most about not having parents is that I would be sent to do difficult chores by anyone feeling like it. I could not refuse no matter how tough the chores were.

Amidst my extended family drama, I was my grandmother's child, sharing a hut with her. I would often be mocked by other children at the playgrounds for being raised under petticoat government, but I didn't care, Gogo was all I had. Although we would often go for days without tea when we ran out of sugar, we were happy in each other's company and that is what mattered.

When mother left home, she was going to look for a job in the city. Communication was not easy those days. When she left, we never heard from her for quite some time until she wrote a letter notifying Gogo where she was. Gogo could not read or write, so I had to read the letter aloud to her. Although we spoke Kalanga more than Ndebele, the letter was written in Ndebele. People spoke Kalanga but for formal communications such as letters, preference was given to Ndebele for some awkward reason.

When people wrote letters to those in the villages, they used the nearest school or store address. Those were the central points where letters were collected. Every Friday, there was a roll call of letters received at school, even those at the store. The senior teacher, who was usually a resident of the village himself, knowing all the villagers, had the responsibility of calling out names. *Mutshu Gumbo*! Gogo's name was called out. I wasn't expecting that name to be called out, so I momentarily froze. Before I could react, Mr Moyo, the senior teacher began asking, *Uyayi Black iwoyu mbsana mfupi ntemantema waka Lungani?* (Where is Black, the short and dark boy from the Lungani clan?). The whole assembly burst in laughter. Eish, the senior teacher's description had awarded the whole school a pass to use my complexion to mock me. I collected the letter and gave it to Gogo still sealed. The letter read:

Kuwe Mama

Kuqala ngibuza impilo, hatshi mina ngiyaphila. Ngibhala incwadi le ngikwazisa ukuthi ngithole umsebenzi ko Bulawayo. Ngizathumela impahla zomntwana nxa ngiholile ukuphela kwenyanga. Ngihlala elokitshini laseMakokoba koBulawayo.

Ubingelele abanye.

Obhalayo yintombi yakho

uSibonile Dube

The letter was simply informing Gogo that mother got a job in the city of Bulawayo, residing at a location called Makokoba. She would send clothes for her son (myself) at the end of the month when she got paid. Oh boy! I was the happiest boy alive. I couldn't wait to wear new clothes. I even forgot that mother had been away for years without communicating. I dreamt about those clothes every day when I went to sleep. Month end came and passed, month ends after that one came and passed too and my dreams began to evaporate.

Children were not included in elderly people's conversations but I overheard that there were lobola negotiations for mother. In fact, suitors were on their way to our village. I had mixed emotions about it. For some reason, I did not want mother to get married because I would not see her quite often. She got married to a man from Chivhu, an area somewhere in Mashonaland. At that time, there were tribal rivalries; it was taboo to cross-marry with the Shona speaking people. I had heard that Shona people had strange traditions especially where marriage is concerned, for instance I heard that if one is married and dies, Shona people get all the property for themselves. I also heard that if a man does not finish paying lobola and the woman dies, they would refuse for the woman to be buried until all lobola is paid.

Everyone was sceptical about mother getting married to a Shona man because of their traditions but no one could refuse her getting married as it was a huge blessing for a woman with a child already to get married. When a woman already had a child, her family would accept whatever form of lobola the in-laws would bring, no matter how small. They would be grateful for the gesticulation in the first place. The ceremony proceedings took place beautifully as if the in-laws were fully welcome. Everyone pretended to be happy and mimicked the Shona language to please the in-laws. After mother left with her Shona people, I did not see her for at least two years or so.

The next time she came to visit, she came with her husband. Gogo had no spare bedroom; as a result, mother had to be spared a hut by one of my uncle's wives. She was given a hut to share with her husband, but my uncle's wife removed all blankets in the room just to fix her. Phela it was every woman's responsibility to buy necessities such as blankets and other household utensils for her maternal home before getting married. Oh boy! Women were always at each other's throat, fixing each other and rejoicing at each other's demise.

Although my maternal family had drama, my alleged father was more dramatic. He became my father only in the classroom. I had never spoken to my alleged father in the first 8 to 10 years of my life until he became my Primary school teacher. He perfectly played his role as a teacher but not as a father. He stayed less than a kilometre from where I stayed but because he had denied fathering me, we had no relations outside the classroom. I had known him from a distance at a younger age since his father was a chief in the area.

I was certain that I resembled him. Perhaps I was imagining things out of my desperate desire to be fathered. Although I was a very sharp learner, somehow I felt that there was an unspoken barrier between us, one that I wouldn't know how to overcome. We seemed to be both bottling words that were forever left unsaid. I desperately wanted to hear his version of the story, but my male pride disallowed me to question him. I would not beg another man to father me. Kids in the classroom were talking about circumstances surrounding my birth. Half-truths and shameful truths. But time would quickly tell my truth.

I came to terms with the fact that I would not stay full time with my biological parents. I accepted reality and felt comfortable in the space that I was in with Gogo by my side and Basekulu (my eldest uncle) taking care of me. In spite of the isolation and condescension that Gogo and I endured from other family members in Basekulu's absence, he would make sure that we were provided for. The problem was that he worked in the city and spent the bulk of his time there. Whenever he came home, he would bring me new clothes and a school uniform. He would make sure that he brought necessities like sugar, soap etc. He never treated me any different from his own children and for that, he became my favourite uncle.

Basekulu fell ill mysteriously and became bedridden in 1972. He was taken to every traditional healer known; but with no success. With Basekulu ailing like that, it meant that I had no school fees, no uniform and we basically could not afford household basics together with his kids. My childhood began to be disrupted slowly.

It was on a cold morning when I received the earth shattering news that Basekulu had died. Yes, I had seen him very sick, but I had not imagined that death could creep in like that. My legs melted below me and I eventually felt my body dissolving to nothingness. I felt like screaming into a hallow world and hear the echo of silence, but my voice disobeyed. I couldn't cry. Emptiness covered me like a cloud. Death had been the only thing powerful enough to snatch my voice. I looked at Gogo and saw astonishment creeping into her face. Imagine losing a son, your own flesh.

People began walking into our homestead as if they were already on standby waiting for such news. I felt like consolers were worsening the situation. The moment they opened their mouths to extend any form of greetings, Gogo and Basekulu's wife would scream like they were possessed. Nothing could take away the emotional torment the whole family was in. I felt a gut-wrenching void of despair because I knew right away that that was the end of my story. The breadwinner was no more. I saw my future vanish before my face. Was I going to complete school? I was 13 years old and in grade 5. That was the beginning of a cold front in my life.

After the catastrophic event that shattered my life, a complication arose and my life and everyone else's in the family changed. It was clear that Basekulu was the thread knitting the entire family together. Everyone in the family started minding their own business. Days would go by without people greeting each other in the homestead. Family members started blaming each other of witchcraft. The once close-knit extended family fell apart. Other uncles started moving out to build their separate homes with their immediate families.

In 1974, two years after Basekulu's death, Gogo and I left our home and built another close by as our larger homestead was now unlivable. Gogo could not live peacefully with her daughters in-law and felt that her authority was undermined as the elderly person in the homestead. Tension was palpable and reached dangerous levels. The only sense-making decision was to build a standalone home. We built a new home at a stone's throw away from our previous one.

We built two grass thatched rondavel houses. At that time, it was easy and less expensive to build a house or home. People depended on *mbizi/amalima* (work parties) where villagers would help each other communally in whatever job and expect no payment in return. Several *mbizi* were held. The first one was strictly for young ladies, it was strictly for fetching water. Ladies would carry water-filled containers on their heads until they filled huge drums that were borrowed for building purposes. The second *mbizi* was for young and elderly men. Their role was to chop logs in the fields that were to be used as poles to support the mud structures and for roofing.

The third *mbizi* was for mature and married women. Their role was to mix the mud and sand to form a thick mortar they used to build the walls. The fourth *mbizi* was for both men and women. Men dug in ridgepoles running parallel to the ground to be used as support structure for the huts and lay the roof rafters together. Women stacked and knit bundles of grass together to form a pattern-like format. The fifth and last *mbizi* was for gentlemen who did the actual thatching, wiring the grass against the laid roof rafters. After the final *mbizi*, the huts were complete at a very low cost. One only had to provide food and beer. All these *mbizi* were hosted at weekly intervals, particularly on weekends.

Although we had built a home of our own, Gogo was aging; she could not do the household chores on her own adequately, like weeding, gathering firewood and fetching water. I had to take over these responsibilities after school and help Gogo out, where I could. I resented everything and everyone around me except Gogo. I had mute contempt towards everyone; my extended family, my father, and mother. Everyone had let me down. I had to develop a thick skin and man up.

Other than family woes, we enjoyed outdoor activities as boys. There were activities such as swimming that no boy could dodge. We were taught how to swim in a gruesome way. Older boys would throw the younger ones into the river pool and leave them until they would nearly drown and then they would dive in, to drag them out just in time before they pass out. The second time they throw you in, you figure out how to swim and get yourself out. Those who were rescued almost late would be resuscitated mouth to mouth and would be beaten on their stomachs using wet sand to compel them to vomit the swallowed water. None of these stories would be conveyed to parents at home. There were consequences for doing so.

In one river pool called Kupa, mysterious things would occur there. Mysterious drowning deaths would take place and bodies would resurface after two weeks. Expert divers would plunge into the pool but not find anything. It seemed as though there was an underworld life in that pool. People could be heard singing, beating drums, whistling and herding cattle, women pounding mealies and so on. It was a mystery that could not be explained. We continued swimming there nonetheless. Unlike other river pools, this one's water was darker and scarier. As we swum, we could somewhat feel the sand underneath coiling our feet and softly dragging us beneath the waters. We were fascinated by this experience as boys, but it was probably this experience that snatched all those who drowned. Because this mystery was normalised and never problematized, as kids, we continued playing there as usual.

Other things we were taught as boys were whistling; calling and directing cattle. Boys who could not whistle were regarded as women or mama's boys raised under women's petticoats. Honestly, to think about it now, the inability to whistle is not a disability at all, it's just like those things other people can or can never do like tongue rolling. In our time, whistling was a symbol of manhood. Older boys would put *umafundakhwelo* (river worm) underneath one's tongue. The belief was that once it bit your tongue, you would instantly start whistling. Some boys were tongue-bitten by umafundakhwelo several times but their tongues resisted.

We went to school barefooted. It was a normal situation for every child. It was nice walking barefooted especially in the rain, our cracked feet would be soaked clean and turn whitish. We loved it; our feet resembled those of White people. We only wore shoes around May and June after the sugar-beans picking season. We would grow a lot of sugar-beans and harvest them in April to be sold to local shops in exchange for tennis shoes. They would last for about 4 months until we each got a new pair the following year.

Although extremely cold, almost every school-going child enjoyed the winter season. Each morning on our way to school, we would watch *mahangaladzimu* (mirage) on the earth's horizon. Every day we saw illusions of different objects, some we had never seen in real life before but in school textbooks. The illusionary objects would stretch from human beings riding on camels, trains, ox-drawn ploughs, ships, cities, raging seas, castles and soldiers at war. Even teachers failed to explain the mystery of the horizon on cold winter mornings. As soon as the sun's rays torched the earth, the illusions would vanish from the earth's skyline.

CHAPTER 2

The journey to Nampundu

had often heard of colonisation, dispossession and displacement but never really thought it would reach us who were residing in the country's peripheries. Our village, Masendu is located in Plumtree, an area bordering two countries: Botswana and Zimbabwe. Its remoteness would have one believe that *Umlungu* (Whiteman) would never set foot there. Besides, what was there to exploit? There were no minerals, no fertile lands and practically nothing worth attracting anyone. Although a very dry region, surprisingly the area is centred on livestock rearing, and thus residents were cattle ranchers and occasionally sold cattle during market days although they were often ripped off at the livestock auctions. Buyers were always *Abelungu* (White men) and sellers of course were the villagers who had very little to no understanding of the monetary concept at that time.

Around the late 1960s, we began to see Abelungu more often in our village even on non-market days. We were not sure what they wanted but we never really crossed paths. It was the first time seeing a person that light in complexion. We had a desperate desire to touch their skin. We wanted to know if they were as human as we were. They spoke so fast, their ears seemed transparent, and that fascinated us. As a result, we called them *Ondlebezikhanyilanga* loosely translating to 'transparent ears'.

One day, it was announced at the school assembly that there was going to be a curfew. We all stood there motionless, as we all had no idea what a curfew was. The headmaster explained that a curfew meant that everyone was to be indoors by 6pm every day and only leave home at 6am the following day. We did not understand the reasons for this curfew but none of us had the audacity to ask the headmaster for clarity. I suspected that it was probably Abelungu's command as two of them stood next to the teachers at the assembly. I suppose that the headmaster was also as nervous and could not ask the reasons too.

We relayed the message to parents. If ever there was any information that needed to be relayed to the village at large, schools were used as channels of communication. The announcement would be made at assembly and learners would convey the message to elders or anyone they meet on their way home. Whenever an elderly person met a school-going child, the first question they would ask was, *Kwayingwi kukwele?* (What announcements were made at school?). Everyone would be up to date with what was happening in the community.

The curfew started, only Abelungu would patrol after 6pm, not certain for what reason. Everyone else was supposed to stay indoors. One weekend we decided to go and dig up a ground beehive I had spotted at the fields across the road. We had to do this quickly before anyone else could spot it and dig up the honey. We were a group of 5 boys and went there around 4pm hoping that we would be back at least before 6pm. The expedition took longer than expected, as the ground was very dry, hence difficult to dig. Before we knew it, it was already darkening.

Just when we were getting ready to go home, we heard two ear-splitting sequential sounds. They were so loud and sharp that I felt as if they cracked my skull. I could not fathom where the sounds came from. Within a few seconds, the sounds echoed back from the Malalume hills to my ears. Queer silence followed and everything seemingly began to move in a slow motion. I had never heard such huge sounds before, but I was gut convinced that they were gunshots.

As soon as I realised that I was still alive, instinctively, I took to my heels without second thoughts. Everyone else fled. Whether the shots were directed at us or not is still a mystery to date. We fled towards whatever direction our feet faced at that moment. Some fled north, east, west and south. Whether we were fleeing towards the direction where shots were made or not was not important at the time, we just wanted to disappear from that field.

We ran towards different directions and lost each other. After 30 minutes of running, I reconnected with my friend Polite towards the homesteads. Our biggest problem was Velempini who was the youngest in the group. Velempini was 9 years old and we couldn't arrive at home without him, worse after those gruesome gunshots that were heard even by people in the 10km vicinity.

How were we going to face and explain to elders at home what had happened to Velempini? While we were strategizing with Polite on what we were going to say to elders, we met an old woman gathering firewood next to her home. We asked if she had seen Velempini. Phew! Velempini had passed by and gone home a few minutes ago. When we arrived home, everyone was talking about the gunshots that were heard from the fields. We could not tell anyone what befell us, as we were not supposed to be out of home during curfew hours.

Was Umlungu hunting or he wanted to shoot at us? But for what reason? We had a lot of questions about curfews, Umlungu's agenda and the shootings. It was unexplainable and people did not want to talk about it. After the curfew incident, the winds of change began to blow. We saw a lot of Abelungu loitering around. Uncertainties were inevitable, people began whispering and different theories emerged. It looked like the beginning of a scary unknown.

Masendu was amongst many villages in the region that sent their cattle Seli, loosely translating to across the river (Thekwane River). Seli was an area reserved strictly as grazing lands for cattle, no homesteads were allowed there. During harvest time, all the cattle were sent Seli to prevent them from grazing on people's crops. Any cow found in one's field meant that the owner would pay a penalty in the form of bags of crops such as maize or sorghum. So, to avoid such penalties, cattle owners drove them Seli.

Most of these cattle would return overnight, craving for fresh crops from the fields. They enjoyed stealing crops more than grazing grass Seli. Nonetheless, villagers looked out for each other, they either sent them back or sent messages to owners if they had seen them returning. People knew each other's cattle, even new-born calves. Each extended family had a unique earmark for their cattle, distinguishing them from others. Whenever an unknown or stray cow was seen, its unique earmark would identify their owners and a word of mouth message would be sent to them.

In 1970, Umlungu called Greenspan was seen pegging and fencing a wide area Seli. This concerned villagers whose cattle grazed there and the matter was reported to the chiefs of the area. Upon consultation, Greenspan indicated that he had bought the farm from the government and produced land ownership documents. As far as local villagers were concerned, the land (Seli) was communal, no one could claim ownership, it belonged to everyone. The villagers lost the case, as they did not produce any document of land ownership. Greenspan had no remorse whatsoever to people he had seized the land from through the protection of the then White government.

Some cattle remained in the area as there were no other grazing lands, they continued wandering around Greenspan's farm. One day a cow was stuck on Greenspan's barbed wire fence and it died overnight leaving a four-day-old calf. This angered villagers, resulting in boys angrily sneaking into the farm to cut the farm's fencing wire. Although this was done incognito, Greenspan had informers. Snitches informed Greenspan of the list of boys who had mischievously cut his fence. The following week, a roll call was made at school of the boys who had cut Greenspan's fence and they were thrashed in front of the whole school by a group of Abelungu.

Soon after the incident, a hut tax was introduced. The hut tax was a type of taxation introduced by the White government on Black villagers. Each household had to pay tax of 50c per month. Other taxes that followed were dog taxes, dip tank tax etc. At this point, the villagers had had enough and were outraged by this costly invasion of their territory.

When we thought we had seen enough, each family's farm was reduced to 5 acres per household by Abelungu. Prior to this, families ploughed on their ancestral lands. It was communally known which land belonged to who, and residents were not selfish, they would lend land to those without or those whose farms were no longer fertile. It was a communal life where people had each other's backs. After farms were downsized, able bodied men were fetched to do contour farming and the reasons for this were never explained.

News began to spread that Black men were leaving the country for training to fight Abelungu who were mistreating Black people and dispossessing them of their belongings. Such news was so scary that people would not publicly talk about, but would meet midnight and whisper about it.

At the time, information became crucial than ever before. We listened to radios. A few households had radios, so we would gather at midnight and listen to the news, particularly about the wave of the armed struggle. We listened to Radio Zambia in particular.

Around 1953, Southern Rhodesia (present day Zimbabwe), Northern Rhodesia (present day Zambia) and Nyasaland (present day Malawi) were amalgamated under one government ruled by the British settlers. The reason for this amalgamation was to strengthen the economic power of the settlers, they would move and exploit freely across the three countries. The federation was finally dissolved 10 years later in 1963 due to political misunderstandings and economic friction amongst the settlers. Southern Rhodesia economically benefited from the federation compared to Northern Rhodesia and Nyasaland. In 1964, shortly after the dissolution, Nyasaland and Northern Rhodesia obtained their independence. Nyasaland became Malawi and Northern Rhodesia became Zambia.

The newly independent countries (Zambia and Malawi) became a beacon of hope for Black nationals of Southern Rhodesia. Thus, radio Zambia was used as a medium of communication and a recruitment platform for Southern Rhodesians to join the war of liberation and fight Abelungu. What fascinated us the most was that, it was Ndebele speaking people who were recruiting us on radio Zambia. One broadcaster said, *"Buya mntwana wekhaya uzothatha isibhamu sakho ulwe laMabhunu"*. This translates to, "Come my fellow countryman and take your gun to fight Abelungu". The voice was so persuasive that any young man listening was charmed by this call. Who does not like to be wooed?

The news about a liberation war boiling up was fascinating to all young men. Other than the desire to fight colonisation, oppression and dispossession, nothing surpassed the thought of owning a gun. We had heard and read enthralling stories about guns. They were going to be the toys we never had growing up. I thought of the gunshot sounds we heard that day at the fields, I imagined myself pulling the trigger and drumming the earth with that thunderous sound. At that moment I knew I wanted to own a weapon, I wanted to be a man.

I had heard stories of the first and second world wars. I knew of one soldier who had fought in the Second World War, although I was not certain of which country he was fighting for. He was respected beyond measure. I actually had a romantic feeling about joining the war. I wasn't the only one, most young men clamoured about the opportunity to be part of the beginning of a history.

After Basekulu passed, I dropped out of school, as I could not afford school fees. It was not out of the ordinary for children to drop out of school before completing their primary education. In fact, half of the learners never completed Grade 7 for various reasons such as failing to pay school fees, heeding to responsibilities such as herding cattle, not having proper clothes, failure to endure beatings by teachers, being dull and general boredom at school.

Through radio Zambia, we learnt that the Zimbabwe African People's Union (ZAPU), a party led by Umdala wethu, Joshua Mqabuko Nkomo was recruiting young people to join the liberation struggle. Some recruits were already in Zambia training for the war. It was, thus, ZAPU leaders who constantly spoke to us on radio Zambia. Joshua Nkomo's party was predominantly comprised of Ndebele and Kalanga speakers residing in Matebeleland and the Midlands regions of the country.

Other than radio recruitment, some recruits would come back from Zambia to forcefully recruit young and able-bodied men from weddings, schools, roadblocks etc. The political, social and economic climate changed. The demand for payment of tax escalated and men were forced to illegally cross borders to neighbouring countries (South Africa and Botswana) to seek employment. Some men were at cross roads, debating on whether they should go seek employment or join the liberation struggle. Most people who were illegally crossing the border into Botswana were arrested by the Tswana and given an option of either deportation back to Southern Rhodesia or being flown to Zambia to train for the war. Botswana had attained its independence at the time and its citizens were in solidarity with Black Southern Rhodesian residents.

Masendu village is a few kilometres away from Botswana, in fact, the distance is walkable, and as a result people would walk to and fro the country. Border laws were not too strict at the time, in actual fact, there was no physical border between Botswana and Southern Rhodesia before 1978, the map was only visually mapped on the ground in 1959 using Maitengwe River as a boundary. The drawing of the map by Abelungu divided people of one tribe, homesteads on the opposite sides of the river fell in different countries, and hence relatives occasionally visited each other across the border.

When I was 17, in 1976, I made up my mind. I wanted to be a man. I wanted to own that AK47, I was determined to do what it takes to elope home and join the armed struggle. I had tried to organise with my friends to cross over to Botswana, but they were cowards, they were scared of leaving their families behind. An opportunity presented itself when I learnt that my neighbour Thubayi was crossing over to Botswana, Mbalambi area to be precise, to visit his girlfriend. I decided to journey with him and told my relatives that I was going to visit my uncle in Botswana.

We woke up in the wee hours of the morning to avoid travelling in the scorching sun. In those days, the earth burnt like hot coals, hence we had to dodge the sun by travelling early morning. The grass was moist with dew that morning; I could only imagine how Thubayi felt, walking bare footed. Thubayi was older than me and quite a naturally timid man, so I did not tell him upfront of my intentions.

Upon crossing Maitengwe River, I intentionally changed my mood and didn't want anything to do with Thubayi. I let him know that I was joining the struggle and he should relay the news back home. He begged me not to, and tried to explain the dangers thereof. As an elderly person, he was worried about breaking such news to my family. Logically, an elderly man is obliged to look after the younger ones. I did not succumb to his plea; I turned a deaf ear and parted ways with him. I was at a point where I could not dodge the call and the desire to free the country, let alone hold and own a gun.

I passed by my uncle's place and disclosed to him of my motive. My uncle begged me not to go and he even offered to assist me attain a citizenship of Botswana and get a good job there. I still did not bend; I was determined and destined to follow my heart. When uncle could not convince me, he gave me money to hike to Francistown and wished me well. When the taxi dropped me off in Francistown, I had no idea of the direction I should take. I stood next to a postman in uniform, so I decided to tell him my case and asked for directions. The postman seemed aware of where I wanted to go and took me there. I shivered upon realising that the postman had taken me to the police station. Deportation was the first thing that came to mind. I resented this man for faking compassion when he was in fact getting me arrested. He initially spoke Kalanga with me but when he handed me over to the police, he spoke Setswana, which I could not understand. Panic was setting in. I was taken to a cell, where I spent the whole night.

To be honest, I could not fathom what had happened. No one explained to me what was going on. I was put in a cell without explanation. I had series of questions that I would ask myself back and forth. Was I being jailed for sure or was that the journey to the unknown, which I had started? There was however, no turning back, a touch was a move.

The following day, a certain Umlungu brought a Black guy from Temateme, my neighbouring village. My understanding of Abelungu was that they were enemies, so how could he recruit freedom fighters to fight fellow Abelungu? That was strange. At that point, I erased the idea that we were still headed for the armed struggle training. Some form of plot twist had happened there, I thought. Surprisingly, beyond greetings, we did not talk much with the new guy in the cell. I was suspicious of him, and I think he was too of me. At 12 midnight, another guy from Kezi arrived. Before dawn, 7 other men arrived from Wenela mines. I regained hope that, that wasn't what my heart of hearts feared the most; deportation and facing the scornful laughter of people back in the village.

In the morning, we were taken out of the cell and had our fingerprints taken. Nothing was explained to us still, we only battled with our thoughts and kept hoping. After the fingerprint session, we were loaded into a police van and driven to an unknown place. One fact I had to accept about the decision I had made was that communication was very limited; we learnt to survive by connecting dots and filling in the missing puzzle.

We finally arrived at a refugee camp in Francistown and met ZAPU leaders and other new recruits. I found out that, not all young men in the camp were voluntary recruits, others were forcefully abducted from schools or any form of public gatherings. At that point, it was clear that the armed struggle was inevitable. We spent about two weeks at that camp waiting for orders of what was to happen to us next. Remember, information of our next move was a scarce commodity, we relied solely on orders, the shape of our tomorrow was very uncertain.

At the beginning of week three, a roll call was made and 120 of us were selected and we were loaded into a convoy of cars and taken to another unknown. We finally arrived at our destination; it was the Francistown airport. It was my first time being at an airport and it was my first time seeing an aeroplane in close proximity but one could not stop wondering what was going on and where we were heading. Matters of the war were sacred even to the participants themselves. Seeing an aeroplane for the first time was an amusement. I marvelled at Umlungu's doing. How could such a huge bird defy the law of gravity?

We boarded a Denmark airline to an unknown destination again. Although everything was still blurry, I gained confidence that we were headed towards the right destination but one could not dodge the distant feeling of mistrust. We discovered our destination upon arrival around 9pm when we saw a sign post written, 'Welcome to Lusaka airport'. At that point I began to connect the dots between radio Zambia recruitments and our destination. It became clear that the newly liberated countries (Botswana and Zambia) were assisting us, Southern Rhodesian freedom fighters to attain our freedom.

Upon arrival at Lusaka, a convoy of Russian Cruz war trucks awaited us. We were struck with nerves when we discovered that Abelungu were driving those trucks. A lot went on in my head. I was not sure whether I should trust them or not. Deep down I thought that was it, they had us and we were dead. I had painted all Abelungu with the same colour paint. Why would the Russians assist Black people? Why did we use a Denmark aircraft? The questions only became food-for-thought at the time, only to be understood at a later stage.

We boarded the trucks and they seemed to be going back and forth aimlessly as if to disguise the enemy. After a while, the trucks off ramped onto a recently graded dust road until we turned onto a bumpy and gulley road that hurt our behinds. The trucks were wide-wheeled, so the drivers paid no attention to the bad road, they drove fast and rough regardless.

After hours of travelling, we began to see lights. That was a point of relief, at least there was a sense of life where we were heading. We finally arrived at our destination, Nampundu camp in Zambia. The camp was securely guarded by armed men. Some hid in the bushes, galleys and on treetops. That day was my first time seeing a gun at a close-up range. Upon arrival at the gate of the camp, we had our names recorded down and we were individually searched to determine if we were not carrying dangerous objects or anything that could be harmful to others.

While we were still completing the checking process, I glanced at group of security guards on the side of the gate. While scanning them, my eyes met my former grade 4 teacher, Mr Bhoyana Ndlovu. I was startled but chose to conceal my discomfiture. I was not expecting to see educated people there. I thought the armed struggle was for us the school dropouts, not people with professional jobs. I wasn't sure if I should greet him or not, so I just stood there immobile and set my eyes off him. Before I knew it, he asked me, '*Mfana uyangazi mina?*' (Young man, do you know me?). I felt a cold front running through my veins. For some reason, I was struck motionless by a kind of paralysis I could not understand. In a split second, my heart began to pound. I had never felt my body change its temperature from normal to cold and eventually hot in less than a minute.

There were two issues, the first one was that we feared our teachers growing up, the only conversation one would have with a teacher was in the classroom. Outside the classroom, we avoided conversations whatsoever with them, in fact, we used to run away from meeting teachers or make a U-turn whenever a teacher was approaching. The second issue was that I wasn't sure of the implications of admitting that I knew anyone in that environment, perhaps it would jeopardise either my stay there or his. The line between an associate and an enemy was blurred under such circumstances.

I staggeringly responded, '*hayi angilazi baba*', (no, I don't know you sir). I was never good with words, I even had a fractured vocabulary especially when I was frightened like that. He responded by saying, 'good'. At that point, I sensed that I said the right response and from that day on, I never saw him. I later learnt that relations were discouraged at the camp. The leaders discouraged people from babysitting their relatives and friends or any form of favouritism. Even blood brothers treated each other like strangers. That was a guerrilla training; men were trained to be fierce and heartless, to kill even those they love. The armed struggle training robbed us of human emotion. We became robotic with no feelings and no emotions whatsoever.

When the registration was complete, we were given two blankets each and a group of security guards divided us to show us our rooms. While journeying towards our rooms, we heard hullabaloo kind of noises; the disturbing noises came from the tall grasses alongside the road. The sounds were akin to that of oinking pigs, we couldn't however see anything as it was midnight. Maybe the camp was self-sustaining after all, rearing own pigs for meat. The security guards off ramped and started walking on tall waist-high grasses. We trailed them although we didn't understand what kind of rooms would be situated on such a grassy area. We discovered that the said rooms were actually that wide grassy area. There were no buildings whatsoever. Good Lord!

We had to find a way of making ourselves comfortable and sleep on that grassy area under the bullet lit sky. This was not what I expected when I left home, but then, there was no turning back. We practically slept in the bush. The oinking sounds of pigs continued throughout the night, only to discover that it were sounds of multitudes of other trainees speaking in whispers through the night. We were informed that in the morning a whistle was to be blown, signalling all trainees to report for parade.

I began to think about how I came to be at that place from my journey with Thubayi. A lot of things actually happened in that short space of time. I began to think if that was even worth it. I thought of Abelungu's rage back home. I began to think that it wasn't that intense after all. Land seizure by Mr Greenspan, the beatings on the buttocks and the hut tax. Other than those, I was oblivious of the other reasons why I would risk my life. The decision I had taken was not for the faint hearted, neither was it for the lily livered. I had not recognised the gravity of my decision and its implications. At that stage, I was in too deep and there was no turning back. After a few seconds of walking in and out of my stream of consciousness vein, I realised that my mind was playing tricks with me. I was beginning to be hysterical. I had to man up and do what it takes to liberate the country.

At exactly 4am, when the whistle was blown, we all jumped and reported for a parade. We had to leave our blankets in our rooms, never mind potential theft or whatever appalling weather condition. We were extremely exhausted from the bumpy road we travelled on, remember we arrived midnight at the camp and slept in the wee hours of the morning.

I had never seen so many people in my life. The camp was as busy and as crowded as an anthill. Even at our primary school assembly, our numbers could not match those at the camp.

At the parade, we were taught all the rules of the camp and from there, all new recruits were told to go welcome and meet Umdala wethu. Umdala was the ZAPU leader Comrade Joshua Nkomo, commonly known as Father Zimbabwe. We were very excited to meet our hero for the first time; we had only heard his voice on radio Zambia. Never had I in my life heard of a man as idolised as Nkomo. He was lionized by his party followers like the Biblical son of God, Christ Himself.

All the new recruits were taken to a nearby hill to meet Umdala. One can map the kind of excitement we had. That was all we ever dreamt of as soon as we decided to join the armed struggle. On the other hand, we were perplexed by why we would meet Umdala up the hill. We soon learnt that Nkomo's helicopter was going to land on that hill for reasons known to himself and his army commanders. Perhaps it would be easier to take cover on the hill surrounded by huge trees in case of an attack. All the new comers walked up the hill to meet Umdala.

The irony about meeting Umdala was that it wasn't meeting him in the actual sense, it was the name of a training exercise where recruits were to frog march and roll down and up the hill. Everything about my journey since the police station saga in Francistown was a mystery beyond comprehension. The confusion was without parallel, everything was unpredictable, and we had to expect the unknown each day.

On my very first day of meeting Umdala, my only pair of khaki trousers got hooked on a tree stump and got torn right at the butt hole, leaving my brown underwear protruding. I stayed for weeks like that, as those were my only clothes. Because I was dark in complexion, people would mistake my underwear for flesh. For that reason, I became a laughing stock and always subjected to mockery by others. Had my grandmother been close, she would have performed magic on my trousers. She would sew them as she did my primary school uniform.

A few weeks after arriving at the camp, we had to change our names and give ourselves war related names to disguise any form of our identities being traced. Names people gave themselves were Struggle, War, Trouble Causer, Snipper, Bazooka etc. My name became Freedom, but my Sotho-speaking friend decided to add a vernacular twist to it and I also became Tokoloho. Tokoloho loosely translates to freedom. I basically used both names at the time. Every trainee had his name changed and most of the armed struggle names became permanent names even after the attainment of freedom.

Nampundu camp was generally inhospitable. We stayed for days without bathing. On the few days we would bath, we would wash at a faraway river without soap or bath towels. The camp was also rat infested. The rats were as big as cats and they would bite our feet when we slept at night. We would wake up to our feet oozing blood. I guess it's true that rats *ngomaluma bephozisa*. They bite you slowly and stealthily such that you may not instantly feel the pain. Besides, we hardly bathed those days so our feet were cracked with a dry and thick brownish accumulating residue such that the rat bite would take time to penetrate.

The issue of not bathing and rats were the least of our problems. The politics of the stomach were a major crisis. We starved to death. The number of people residing at that camp was beyond ridiculous; hence, our leaders failed to provide enough food for everyone. Our meals were largely a small portion of pap with either carpenter fish or beans. The situation trained our bodies to hold small amounts of food.

Other than the meagre amounts of food served, the dining conditions were extremely pathetic. We ate with our soiled hands. There was no water in the camp to wash hands. We drank contaminated water straight from dams and rivers. People would get mouth blisters from the unhygienic conditions and others succumbed to diseases such as diarrhoea and cholera. Those who succumbed to diseases and died would be unceremoniously buried like animals without dignity and any form of a formal send off. Life would move on normally as if nothing happened and families back home were never informed.

When we eventually got accustomed to the place, we started doing *mawela* (washing our plates and queueing for food again unnoticed). The kind of food served was so unpalatable that it could not appetize the hungriest or greediest of jackals. The situation reduced us to hungry scavengers. We ate anything we could, from edible tree leaves, edible roots and insects. We even slaughtered owls. That's creepy, isn't it? We threw away the owl's head and ate the body. Our motto when it came to owls was that an owl is the head; the rest of the body is chicken. Simple! Once you remove the head, nothing reminds you that it's an owl.

When new recruits came in, we would take advantage of them and force them to give us their shares of food. Drought not only meant hunger, but it turned to inhumanity and meant anger too. We became animalistic towards our fellow brothers just to satisfy our ever growling and howling stomachs. In the words of Thabo Mbeki, we had certainly lost our sanity, because to be sane (in such circumstances) was to invite pain.

As time went by, I began to see familiar faces. It seemed as though all the able-bodied men from my village were there. Some of them were forcefully and involuntarily recruited after I had left. I also learnt that women were also recruited and abducted in some instances, and they had their own separate women camp where they were trained.

We made friends with people from other regions and started to secretly interact with villagers, selling our blankets and exchanging cigarettes for food. One thing the camp had a huge supply of, were cigarettes. Whether we smoked or not, we were given two boxes per week. It were those boxes that we barter traded with villagers for food. We trained at Nampundu camp for six months. In July 1977, 2400 trainees were selected and we were to be sent to another unknown. I was amongst those.

CHAPTER 3

Boma: Escaping death by a centimetre

From more than 10 000 trainees at Nampundu camp, 2400 able bodied and medically fit young men were selected and I was amongst them. We were to be moved to a different location, but the details were never disclosed. Moving to an unfamiliar place always trembled one. Although the living conditions were appalling, we had somehow gotten comfortable at Nampundu. We had built strong relations with neighbouring villagers who often sympathised with us and gave us food. We also had girlfriends whose only purpose was to fulfil our sexual desires. We had no connection whatsoever with those women other than sexual favours. We would easily not master their names; as long we knew their location, we were good. We would sneak out of the camp midnight to visit our girlfriends who often shared huts with their siblings or relatives. We would make our usual signals like whistling and a girl would stealthily tip-toe out of the homestead if chance allowed. We would enjoy each other's company in the bushes and immediately part ways when the mission was accomplished.

The day we were all dreading finally came. A convoy of more than 50 Russian army Cruz trucks ferried us from the camp, heading to the unknown. Other cars transported food and others carried equipment and weapons. Although at Nampundu we were trained largely by Russians, this time we were ferried by the Cubans. As soon as the car engines roared, we were all engrossed in deep thoughts thinking about the unknown laying ahead of us. Nobody was talking to anyone; the journey was a dead silent one. Other than not knowing where we were headed, the thought of why the Cubans were involved remained a momentary mystery. I was not accustomed to the politics of the world, hence a lot of questions flashed in my mind. At that point, I guess we accepted the life of being transported from point A to B like cargo without either consent or explanation and negotiation.

The journey took about 6 days, although we would stop to eat and rest along the way. We later learnt that we were headed to Boma camp near Lusu in Angola. Boma was a camp set up to train ZAPU freedom fighters who had completed their first phase of training in Nampundu, Zambia. However, these camps were not permanent bases; they could be abandoned once there was a realisation that the enemy (the Rhodesian forces) found out about them. There were several other camps that were there in Zambia for instance, that were mercilessly bombed by the Rhodesian forces in an attempt to disarm freedom fighters.

Immediately we set foot in Angola, I fell in love with the country. The scenery was different and eye catching. Of all the African countries I had been to, Angola had the most beautiful landscape with dense luxuriant vegetation, and ever flowing rivers. Its soil looked very fertile and rich that any plant could effortlessly grow on it.

Frogs could be heard singing jubilation songs in nearby streams. The sky was made alive by the chirping melodies of insects and decorated with colourful butterflies. Millions of birds hovered the sky, hawking on insects that seemed far from depletion. The scenery was just a beautiful sight.

We arrived at the camp at twilight on the 6th day. As usual, the first process was registering our names and thorough individual searching was done. Just like at any army base, there were fears of potential armed intruders or sell-outs masquerading as locals or trainees and bombing the camp incognito. Registration took place and was completed by midnight. We were escorted to our residences. I was delighted to learn that this time around we would have shelter over our heads. At least the camp had tents where we would sleep in, although we shared in huge numbers. What mattered the most was having a roof over our heads.

The first and most important rule of each of these camps was that every morning at 4am, everyone assembled for a parade. Dodging parade was a punishable offence and leaders would deal with the lawbreaker accordingly. Despite having slept late, at 4am the following day we heeded the parade call. Just like at Nampundu, there were so many people. It was multitudes of men. The number outweighed that of trainees at Nampundu. It was as if all young Black men of Southern Rhodesia were there. This liberation movement was no joke, it was indeed greater than I had imagined. Abelungu had no chance.

I saw familiar faces of people who had joined the armed struggle way before I did. However, a few days after we arrived, the preceding group that trained and completed before us was being moved to another undisclosed location.

At Nampundu we were taught general war tactics and did a lot of physical exercises. The training at Boma was however more intense, focusing largely on military strategies such as the guerrilla warfare by the Cubans and the Russians.

Our dreams came true the day we were each handed an AK-47. Many of us joined the struggle to fulfil our desperate desire to own, let alone handle a gun. At that point, the training we received centred on shooting, snipping and operating huge machine guns such as the Dakota and setting up bombs. Other than the physical and machine operating trainings, we were also taught political tactics and being vigilant all the time. The first rule when it came to guns was that losing one was equal to a death sentence. Trainees and freedom fighters would rather commit suicide than report a gun missing. A soldier would rather die at a war than lose their weapon and reporting back empty handed. That was Joshua Nkomo's policy and it ought not to be broken.

One traumatic yet non-negotiable ritual of the camp was punishment. We were handed severe punishments even for committing trivial offenses such as arriving late for a parade, being caught hunting or interacting with villagers. Punishments were generally inevitable. It was not possible to spend a week without earning a punishment. Any silly deed landed one in trouble, even the ones we were not aware were punishable offences like strolling aimlessly in the camp.

Boma camp was home away from home; the living conditions outweighed those at Nampundu by far and were not as appalling. Upon arrival, we were given soap and razors to cut our hair. At Nampundu we never got to cut our hair, we had no equipment to do so. As a result, our coiled unkempt hair was a breeding ground for whatever small insects there was and it was lice infected. At Nampundu we rarely washed, on few instances we did, we did so without soap. As a result, the lice infestation was so severe that we ended up having no hair at the backside of the head. The lice would feed off the bottom of the scalp, resulting in this baldness.

The diet at the Boma camp was heavenly compared to Nampundu. We ate barley rice, tinned food, drank chocolate tea with condensed milk and had buns for breakfast. Even the food portions were sizeable. I remember on two separate occasions where we had elephant and crocodile meat. Both the mammal and reptile had this unique yet incongruent tongue tickling meat, tasting half-fish, half-chicken and half-pork. The crocodile in particular had delicious tender munchable bones that swell softly in one's mouth. I enjoyed it.

The only issue we could not cope with at Boma was the Angolan weather. The country is situated in the Southern hemisphere and some of its regions that are in proximity with the equator have abundant rains. It rained almost every day and we had to undergo intense training under such humid conditions. One thing I found intriguing about the country was that fruits like mangoes grew as wild fruits. They easily grew in the wild and we would pick and harvest whenever we felt like. I have never in my life enjoyed mangoes like I did in Angola. They came in different sizes, shapes and tastes.

Since the camp was huge and had a large number of people, for manageability reasons, we were divided into companies (large groups). Each company had 160 people. Each company was further divided into 5 platoons (squads). I was allocated to company 8. Each company had a Cuban or Russian leader and platoon leaders were selected amongst trainees.

Our company 8 leader, Pit Bull made our lives a living hell with his boiling temper. He was a Cuban disfigured giant man with a grotesque shaped hunchback. He was nick named Pit Bull because of his gruesome and abnormally curved verte-bral. The fella was extremely mean. We logically concluded that he was bullied in his childhood because of his physical deformity and adopted meanness as a coping strategy. He had weirdly huge jaundiced eyes. His stare and glance during trainings sent people scampering with activity and bumping onto each other in fear.

He always had a theatrically thunderous voice crescendo and he shouted at us pitching his voice as if he was addressing partially deaf primary school children at assembly. Whenever he spoke, we strategically took cover as violent squirts of saliva gushed out to waterlog his mouth, showering those in proximity. The sight of him generally sent trainees into mass depression.

Three months down the line, the camp became inhospitable. Food potions began to dwindle and the environment generally turned unhygienic. Food and toiletry supplies ran out. We started asking for food from villagers incognito, as we were not allowed to have any interaction with them.

Angolan villagers were very welcoming although language was often the barrier as most civilians spoke Portuguese. We also traded cigarettes, matches and soap with villagers for cassava and other food items. All the schools around had food schemes, so we secretly went to ask for food. Although there were people frequently spying on us, the general population understood our predicament.

Angola had recently attained its independence, so most residents were aware of what it takes to support a fellow Black man fighting for independence. We later learnt that the food crisis was caused by the Rhodesian army. Apparently, upon discovering the locations of freedom fighters' camps in Angola and Zambia, the Rhodesian army blocked any form of supplies from reaching the territories. They bribed villagers in Zambia and Angola for any information.

When living conditions worsened, some form of typhoid hit the camp. Almost half of the trainees fell sick. As a child, growing up, I don't remember falling sick, let alone suffer from any kind of ordinary sicknesses like headache, flu or tummy ache. We grew up chewing a certain herb called *intolwane* that our grandmothers gave us often. Intolwane was said to make us physically strong and had a nutritional power to protect and prevent us from falling sick. We were in a foreign land and could not get intolwane.

Although I dodged typhoid for about a month, my body eventually lost its defences and gave in. I started with flu-like symptoms such as headache, occasional cold and numbness.

Sickness was generally new to me; I had never felt like that before. At first, I ignored the symptoms and tried to strengthen my body with harsh exercises but my system weakened and couldn't hold up anymore. When the flu-like symptoms subsided, my tummy attacked me, it started having intense cramps; I could neither eat nor stand on my feet. My stomach flipped over and knotted such that I would only feel a bit of comfort when I was down on my knees. I was bedridden for several weeks until I was finally taken to a nearby hospital.

Public hospitals' atmosphere was, in most cases generally covered with an unsettling and hair-raising cloud. I vividly remember the day I was wheeled in, on a stretcher. The hollowness of the hospital corridor didn't pronounce life but lifelessness. I felt as if I was being escorted to death. In fact, the corridor smelt of death, never mind the fact that I had no idea how death smelt like. When I finally laid on my hospital bed, I looked around the ward and what did I see? The sight of an overpopulated ward filled with frail and debilitated patients sleeping on narrow hospital beds made my heart knock at my ribs. I did not see myself surviving in such an environment, it aroused a feeling of helplessness and I felt like my hourglass had run out of sand. As days went by, all hope of life dwindled as my body weakened to a typical state of lifelessness. I felt like I was dying a slow death.

I was admitted in the hospital for a weeklong period. No one from the camp was allowed to come to the hospital for visits. On the second week, I began feeling much better. My stomach cramped no more; I only felt a sense of weakness, I guess emanating from laying too long on the bed. To everyone's surprise, I miraculously recovered, dodging death by a centimetre. After recovering, I spent another week at the hospital as no one came to check on the hospitalised or ferry the recovered. An opportunity presented itself when two other trainees were brought to the hospital. That is when I got transport back to the camp.

When I returned back to the camp, I learnt that my close friend Mbuli had died of typhoid before he could be taken to the hospital. Shiver went up my spine. I caught the cold immediately. When I was hospitalised, Mbuli was one of the people who carried me to the car and made sure I lay comfortably. I vividly remember him cushioning my neck with one of his blankets, which he probably never got back. My greatest concern was that I could not publicly mourn him; it was a sign of weakness under the circumstances we were in. We were training to be guerrillas, we had to be animalistic and conceal any form of sorrow. I mourned for my friend in solitude. The masses of trainees who died of typhoid were buried like dogs without mourners' present.

After spending a few months at Boma, one could not help but observe that Pit Bull was prematurely ageing overnight. Something was clearly eating him from the inside. He soon disappeared from the public eye and our company was put under new leadership. News soon spread that Pit Bull succumbed to a spine disease, which he periodically suffered from, since childhood. Although we despised him and his leadership techniques, death could never sit well with anyone. After all, he had sacrificed his precious family time and opted to live under those hazardous conditions, training Black people he had no connection with, whatsoever. It was at that moment that we started valuing the time he sacrificed for us. It's a pity that it was too late to express our gratitude. I guess we never know good until it's gone. Death be not proud!

We enjoyed swimming and taking baths in Angolan ever-flowing rivers. The country is very rich in oil with the second largest oil reserves in the continent. Its soil was glittering with smidgeons of oil and rivers contaminated with small droplets of oil. It was difficult to find pure water purified from oil.

*　*　*

At the time, Angola was a newly independent country previously colonised by Portugal. The country had earned its independence in 1974. At the time, independent African countries were largely in solidarity with those still colonised. The ultimate Pan African goal was to assist in the freedom of all African Nations. Although Angola attained freedom from Portugal, its internal politics continued and later intensified into a civil war. The civil war was a power scuffle between two former freedom fighters who fought the Portuguese: the communist People's Movement for the Liberation of Angola (MPLA) and the anti-communist National Union for the Total Independence of Angola (UNITA).

Although the two parties previously had a shared aim of liberating Angola, their civil war lasted for more than two decades after the country's liberation. Their scuffle was almost akin to the political earthquake soon to unfold in Zimbabwe between the two nationalist major parties involved in the armed struggle; Zimbabwe African People's Union (ZAPU) led by Joshua Nkomo and Zimbabwe African National Union (ZANU) led by Robert Gabriel Mugabe. MPLA supported our cause, and it is the party that had welcomed us in the country and provided a camp base. UNITA was in opposition as the party was being promoted and supported by the White South Africans who were also in alliance with the Southern Rhodesian forces back home.

The irony about most armed African wings in each country was that, although fighting the common enemy, the coloniser, each wing had support from different countries. While ZAPU freedom fighters trained in Zambia and Angola, ZANU freedom fighters trained in Mozambique and some parts of Zambia.

Mozambique had gained independence from Portugal in 1975. Just like Angola and Zimbabwe, a civil war took place in the country between parties that had fought for independence against Portugal. The two major parties were the Front for Liberation of Mozambique (FRELIMO) and Mozambican National Resistance (RENAMO). The White South Africans and Southern Rhodesians backed RENAMO to resist FRELIMO, which supported other black Nationalists towards their independence. In simple terms, White South Africans and Southern Rhodesians White forces stirred civil wars in newly independent countries by puppeteering one nationalist party against the one supporting their countries' armed struggle.

The Zimbabwe African National Liberation Army (ZANLA), a ZANU's armed wing was backed by China, while the Zimbabwe People's Revolutionary Army (ZIPRA), a ZAPU's armed wing was supported by the Soviet Union (Russia). The Cubans in Angola assisted in training ZAPU freedom fighters as they were already in the country supporting MPLA against interventions by White South Africans and their alliances who opposed the idea of African countries' independence, lest it spread to their country.

Our group spent six months in Angola. On the sixth month, we were flown back to Zambia to another camp, different from the one we were residing in before. When we left Boma, another group of trainees arrived. The idea of having different camps for training was that we could not afford being in one place at the same time, lest we all succumb to massacres by the enemy simultaneously.

CHAPTER 4

Zambezi River and the gun

FRELIMO was a Mozambique Liberation Front, fighting for Mozambique's freedom from the Portuguese. Their war of independence started in 1964 and ended in 1974, with Black freedom fighters gaining a landslide victory. During the Mozambican liberation, FRELIMO trained its freedom fighters in Zambia, which had gained its independence in 1964. FRELIMO had established a training camp in Zambia called the FRELIMO Camp (FC) during their liberation struggle. At Mozambique's independence, FRELIMO deserted their Zambian camp. It was at this camp that we stayed and trained after leaving Boma in Angola. FRELIMO Camp was also known as the Freedom Camp (FC).

On one fateful day after completing an intensive training, my friends and I decided to go hunting. We escaped the camp unnoticed at midnight. Although we were not allowed to leave the camp without instruction from the supervisors, we were now *inja zegame* (dogs of the game), having mastered all the tactics of escape. In some instances, we went as far as negotiating with the security guards or bribing those that we were not familiar with, whenever we needed to go out. We hunted for any wild animals we came into contact with, to supplement meals at the camp. A successful catch meant that we would braai meat overnight and eat as much as we could for the days to come because meals came in small quantities at the camp. The situation taught us to instinctively learn to fend for ourselves and supplement meals, as long as we were not caught.

During our hunting expeditions, we usually shot hares, kudus, impalas and any other small animals whether their meat was edible or not. Times were tough. When we caught huge animals like Kudus, we would share with villagers we had established friendships with, and they would dry up the meat for us to eat at a later stage. FC was situated not far from the Zambezi River. In order to catch night animals, we would hide in reeds and tall grasses close to the riverbank and wait for them to bow into the river to drink water and we would shoot at them. Amongst other hunting tactics, this is how we largely caught our prey.

On that fateful night, we spotted and waited for a herd of Impalas to approach the riverbank. It was mind blowing watching wild animals checking the coast before bowing to drink from the river. They would stare into the river for a long time as if to check if there wasn't any form of danger or predators. Wild animals like Impalas seemed to have a dis-tinguished sharp sense of hearing. They would pay attention every time there was any small movement or sound in the vicinity. They would lift their ears every time they were about to drink water to pay attention to any unfamiliar movement or sound. I guess they knew that they could be preyed on either by land or water predators, off guard, as they bowed their heads.

When the herd of Impalas had finally let their guard down and started drinking water, I exercised my sniping skills I had trained for in Angola, shooting an Impala, which immediately fell to its feet within a second. The gunshot sound sent the larger herd scampering towards whatever direction; others slipping into the crocodile infested river. I can only imagine the fate of those that fell into the river, infested with hungry scavengers.

I had to act fast to pick my kill before crocodiles could pull it into the river and feast on it. The Impala had fallen such that its head and neck were hanging into the river. With the way the river bank was moist, the animal could easily succumb to the law of gravity and slide into the river. I caught it by its legs, with my gun under my armpit and tried to pull the beast from the riverbank. While at it, I caught sight of a gigantic crocodile stealthily swimming towards me. A momentary blackout happened to my consciousness; I lifted my arm trying to pull my prey fast towards me and escape the reptile. At that moment, I had not realised that I let go of my gun and it slid into the river. When my senses came back, I almost soiled myself. Of all the days I have and yet to live in my life, that was the worst.

I made a loud piecing scream that echoed through the night. My friends had no idea of what had just happened as they stood further than I was, while this happened. I'm sure in their minds, they were busy strategizing about where we would braai our meat. My first instinct signalled me to throw myself into the river to be ripped by the crocs at once and meet my ancestors. According to the ZAPU laws, it was taboo to lose a gun. A gun was more important that human life, in fact we were taught to rather sacrifice ourselves at war than to lose a gun. For instance, it was considered heroic bringing a deceased's gun together with yours, than returning empty handed after a clash with the enemy.

When my friends learnt about my fate, they knew they were also in trouble. There was no way this expedition would go undetected. We obviously had to report the incident and they would not distance themselves from such a huge offense. I suggested throwing myself into the Zambezi River, but they wouldn't let me. Mgambari suggested that I cross over to

Southern Rhodesia and just disappear without trace. Sgonondo disagreed with the idea of running away. He pinpointed that my disappearance was a threat to the entire army and I would be traced down as a sell-out suspect to be eventually killed mercilessly. I also knew that if I ran away, members of the intelligence department would sniff until they got information about our midnight camp escape. Mgambari and Sgonondo would be in trouble, they would even be slain for concealing such information. We tried to look into the river to check if the gun was not visible. The water was as dark as the night itself, nothing could be seen except a bask of crocodiles wrestling with each other, fighting over an impala's carcass.

We decided against suicide and fleeing. We were going to report the incident to authorities and face the consequences. The journey back to the camp was a very quiet one. Each one of us was battling with their thoughts, concocting a plan of how we would explain the incident. I was a walking zombie; my body was numb as if it was struck by some kind of a paralysis. All I could do was to drag my feet and go meet my fate. I would soliloquise along the way, thinking about why I hadn't left my gun with Mgambari and Sgonondo when I went to pull the dead impala from the riverbank. Why would a grown ass man put a gun under an armpit? Was the crocodile approaching viciously that I could not escape it, had I not panicked? My life was just a catalogue of disasters; I guess I needed some form of ceremonial cleansing.

We had even left the beast by the river and forgot about it. Upon arriving at the camp, we firstly reported the incident to the security guards we had bribed. We didn't want to put them in any trouble, hence we had to strategize with them the narrative we were going to stick with. The whole incident immediately sent them to depression and they blamed themselves for allowing us to leave the camp. A mere apology was not even enough for smearing them with so much trouble.

We finally agreed that we were to exclude their involvement in our saga and we were to stick to the story that we jumped over the fence.

At that point, we were not sure of who to report to. It was midnight; we couldn't wake army commanders from their sleep. Although we were aware of the hierarchical structure of our armed wing, the gravity of our incident sent shivers to our spines, thus we decided to dodge hierarchy and protocol by reporting to Makhabharetha who led Sgonondo's platoon. Mgambari and I were in a platoon led by Ndazi. Makhabaretha was approachable and soft-spoken compared to Ndazi who gave us nightmares with his ruthlessness and was always as vicious as a volcanic lava. When we broke the news to Makhabharetha, he was equally troubled. He didn't know how he was to report the matter to his leaders. He suggested that we report to Ndazi as the missing gun was mine, not his subordinate's.

The thought of approaching Ndazi sent quivers to our bodies. He was going to be as dramatic as a soap opera. We tried to convince Makhabharetha to take up our case to relevant authorities and try to sweet talk them. He eventually gave in and sent us to sleep, as he was to report early in the morning. We were not sure if sleeping was the right thing to do with a missing gun. The gravity of this crime deserved to be dealt with instantly. We decided not to challenge Makhabharetha's decision and retired to sleep.

None of us could sleep that night; we turned and tossed all night long. Just when I finally dozed off to sleep, the parade whistle rang. I was just in the moment of trying to forget what befell me the previous night and the whistle took me back to that fateful incident I was trying to escape from. When we reported to the parade, our incident was the talk of the camp. We were called by authorities to explain what had happened. I naturally had speech problems, so I tried to articulate what had transpired but stammered as words evicted themselves out of my mouth. While at it, one of the commanders lost patience and got irritated by my speech deformity. He bellowed at me to shut up and asked Sgonondo to reiterate what had happened.

Sgonondo was an overly dramatic and highly active young man who always spoke in slang and used a lot of hand gestures for emphatic purposes. He would pitch his voice where there was a need to dramatize an incident and speak with softness when he was buying sympathy. Although he was more eloquent than I was, his choice of words and slang was just not appropriate for explaining such a serious incident. He was likely to add fuel to flames, jeopardise the case and worsen the already critical situation.

Sgonondo:

Bahlonitshwa, okwenzakeleyo yikuthi besibanjwe liphango labafowethu. Besingazange sisuthe emdanyane. Manje sathi plan ban? Sathi weliyani ngale ko cingo lwe nkampa sisithi singathola okokuwosa. Sanyonyoba saze sayawela emfuleni sitymele okuyiznanakazana kobusuku sokusiyanatha. Sithe sisithi syathi, ahhh thutshiyani umhlambi wempala. Thixo wase Nazaretha, inhlanhla engaka! Thina cathamiyani emihlangeni eceleni komfula. Sazilinda impala zawela. Zithe zisithi khothamiyani, umfwethu waluthela uhlamvu, eyi 1 yahle yaya kogoqwanyawo. Ezinye zithe zisizwa umdumo wesibhamu vele zasabalala zagcwala indawo yonke. Ezinye zahle zabhukutsha vele emfuleni zihlangabezana lengwenya zilambe over. Ngokuphazima kweso kwasokuyisisana sana umtshado wezinja, amanzi aba ligazi, ingwenya zizitika. Bekungasi ngwenya bekufiwa laphayana. Umfwethu weqa vele wayathatha impala yakhe eyayilengele emanzini. Uthe

*ethi uyayidonsa, wathi mehlo suka emanzini. Ahh!
vumbulukiyani inkalakatha yengwenya ingagqize
qhakala. Uthe ethi uyahlehla, isbhamu gqum emanzini.
Yhooooo, Yeso Khristu ndodana kaDavida! yinto
ezathiwani le? Phela simbambe esezilahlela emfuleni
kayi 1, sathi kungcono siyekhulumisana labafowethu
abangabakhokheli. Phela umuntu kalahlwa ephila.*

We all paid attention to this dramatic tale articulated by
Sgonondo. I wasn't sure what to make of his dramatization. I
tried to weigh the reception of this story on the commanders'
eyes but could not determine. But deep down I felt like his
articulation had eased the situation. After that, he stood there
fidgeting like a toddler, while I was as motionless as a statue.
The commanders decided to give us a severe punishment. We
were to dig a dungeon three feet deep and three feet wide in
three days. Once we were done, we were to report completion
and another punishment would follow.

Although this was a huge punishment, I was grateful that I
was alive. Losing a gun was synonymous to a death warrant.
I had escaped death. We dug the dungeon and at night, our
friends would join in to secretly help us. Little did I know that
I was digging my own grave.

After three days, we reported completion to authorities
who came to inspect. We were then asked to pour buckets of
water into the dungeon and cut logs to place them over the
dungeon to cover it up. Once we completed those tasks, my
accomplices were excused while my punishment continued.
I was put in that dungeon to stay and sleep there while water
was constantly poured over me. I could not sleep for days,
imagine the muddiness inside and having to relieve myself in
the same place I slept in. Food was brought to me inside the
dungeon. At that point, I felt like death was actually better
than that torture.

I stayed underground in solitude for about three weeks. I realised that every day we are given a choice, to be grateful of life or despair and die. I chose to live even under such circumstances. Sgonondo, Mgambari and a few of my friends were apparently restless about my case. They decided to consult a well-known traditional medicine man called Kawanga from the nearby Zambian village. Absolutely nothing was beyond Kawanga's fix; his influence would stretch as far as bordering villages in Southern Rhodesia. So, when Kawanga was consulted, he asked what oSgonondo wanted him to do for them. They explained to him what had transpired for me to be detained in that dungeon, and therefore asked him to perform whatever miracle he could to have me released. He asked them to go and show him the spot where the incident had happened by the riverbank.

He asked them to come back after three days with payment; he would have performed his miracle. OSgonondo did not have any cash, so they sold their blankets, cigarettes and matches to villagers in order to pay Kawanga his dues. On the fourth day, they reported to Kawanga's hut and paid his dues hoping for the said miracle. Kawanga accepted the payment but said nothing about what he had performed. One could not begin to ask the medicine man about what was going on; they just had to wait for him to inform them.

Kawanga started burning some kind of traditional incense, throwing bones onto his reed-made-mat and began speaking to his ancestors. After a few minutes of speaking in an unknown language akin to the Biblical tongues, Kawanga took them to the river, precisely the spot where the incident took place. Upon arrival, he spread his mat and started consulting his ancestors again. He then removed his sandals and plunged into the crocodile infested river. Jesus Christ! Kawanga disappeared into the water for about 20 minutes.

According to Sgonondo and crew, they didn't know whether he would make it alive or not. They were all struck by confusion, but kept on seeing bubbles on the spot where Kawanga had plunged. After 20 minutes, Kawanga reappeared holding the AK-47 that had fallen into the river about three weeks ago. Everybody stood there wide-eyed, believing that their eyes were deceiving them. Zambezi is the fourth largest river in Africa, not only wide but extremely deep. How could the man dive to the deep bottom of that river? Sgonondo and crew brought the gun and I was immediately released from that dungeon. Wonders never ceased to happen, I am forever grateful to Kawanga, Sgonondo, Mgambari, Sitha and Matshayinyoka. I soon learnt that Sgonondo's ridiculous storytelling had saved my ass from being beheaded. According to the commanders, I was given a light punishment compared to the gravity of my delinquency. ACCORDING TO ZAPU LAWS, YOU DO NOT DARE LOSE A GUN.

A month after that nightmarish incident, we were summoned to attend a parade and we were informed of the coming of Umdala. This time around, the coming of umdala was real; it wasn't the fresher training we had received at Nampundu about a year ago. Everyone was appointed a responsibility. I was appointed to be a security guard waiting to receive Umdala at the base, further away from the camp. After a year of training, welcoming and protecting our hero and leader was the best thing one could ever do.

We wore our military gear made of camouflaged material. Most military uniforms had camouflage textiles to protect soldiers from observation by the enemy. Even our military equipment and vehicles had a camouflage, khaki or army green colour to conceal them from easy identification and observation by the opponent. A soldier in uniform could easily look like a tree trunk or could hideout behind a tree or lie flat on the grass unnoticed. Visual deception has always been a war trick. Even Abelungu would, in some instances smear their faces with coal to resemble Black people and wear the opponent's uniform to disguise and pretend to be a part of them and strike unobserved. The coal-smearing however, made them to look ridiculous close-up.

We took cover around 4pm and prepared for the great coming of our leader. Others lay in the trenches strategically dug for war purposes in case the enemy decided to strike. Although this wasn't war, there was need to protect Umdala. Nothing was certain at the time; even the enemy could not sleep plotting to destroy us. Sell-outs were also rampant at the time; the climate had changed and the war was in progress in Southern Rhodesia. Those who had trained before us were already on the frontline of the battle in the country and it had reached its intensity.

Towards 6pm, helicopters lit the sky and we panicked momentarily. We were not expecting so many aircrafts. Through the radio overs (ova-ova), our commanders assured us that Umdala was being escorted by other military helicopters for safety reasons. In case of a helicopter shoot down, the enemy would not know which of the many transported the leader and the common stunt generally increased the security of the official being transported. A person as important as Umdala had to be accompanied by other spotting aircrafts to observe the enemy on the ground.

While we were at the base, further than the camp, undercover and awaiting Umdala's arrival, we spotted the planes starting to fly at tree top level close to the camp. Within a fraction of a second, hell broke loose and bombs started raining from the sky producing lightning-like earth-shattering blasts, hitting the camp one after the other. We lay motionless like witches at our base and trenches while the aircrafts continued dropping scores of bombs at the camp.

Good Lord! We had not seen all that coming. The aircrafts we thought transported Umdala actually belonged to the enemy. Questions rang in our minds. What had happened? Where did communication go wrong? Were there sell-outs in our midst? How could the trusted intelligence unit be disguised like this and miss such a glitch? Within few minutes, the camp was enveloped by a thick dark cloud of smoke, but that did not stop the enemy from dropping bombs. We definitely had sell-outs right under our noses, but who?

The bombing went on at FC for about two hours. At first, we watched the merciless dropping of bombs by the enemy. Generally, there was an atmosphere of fretfulness; we were not ready for such a kind of attack. After recovering from this shock, we began communicating with the commanders of the way forward but we became suspicious of each other and couldn't trust anyone amongst ourselves. We were not sure of the person who had links with the enemy, it was obvious it was one of the top leaders and the person was obviously amongst us at the base. Most definitely, he would not risk his life by remaining at the camp.

At the base, a troop of soldiers hid at the trenches including myself, while others watched events unfold on top of the hill. We decided to tiptoe and zigzag up the hilltop to join our comrades and decide the way forward. At the hilltop, there were 3 anti-air guns and we had 4 battalions that engulfed about 6 companies. However, our anti-air guns had no enough ammunition to shoot down the enemy's aircrafts.

Our commander took a risk amidst the dangerous commotion, sneaked out, hiked and went to fetch weapons in Lusaka where our head quotas were. There were about 24 enemy helicopters flying above the vicinity. We had a strela-2, a surface to air missile launcher that could detect and follow the engine of an aircraft. After about one hour 30 minutes, the army commander brought the necessary equipment. We decided to retaliate and shoot down the Rhodesian army's aircrafts. We caught sight of a helicopter climbing up after dropping a bomb. Our comrade Bhiva responded by firing a missile which narrowly missed the tail of the aircraft by few centimetres. Panic arose as that was the gravest mistake one could commit of miscalculating and missing the target.

The enemy responded by sending a Dakota aircraft towards the direction where the missile was fired. When the Dakota was flying in between our camp and our base, Bhiva fired a missile that tailed the aircraft, hitting its belly and ripping it apart in few seconds. Both the ripped parts; the cockpit and the tail immediately caught fire, spun down and plunged to the ground simultaneously. For us, that was a moment of celebration; we even left our bases and joined each other in celebration. That was an achievement, it was the first time taking down Umlungu's aircraft.

The bombing operation lasted for several hours. Although we had taken down the Dakota, our comrades perished at the camp. With the way the bombs were raining down, it was obvious that the camp was now in ruins. Fire engulfed the whole area; and it became a sorry sight. All we could do was to watch helplessly from the hill-top, we were not prepared for that kind of war. Most of our weapons perished in the camp. I shivered from head to toe, realising my narrow escape. Had I not been appointed as a security guard to await Nkomo at the base, I also would have perished.

The operation lasted for several hours at FC. After the FC massacre, when everything was shattered and in ruins, the enemy shifted attention to Mkushi camp. Mkushi was a ZAPU sister camp strictly for training women. It was located about 150km North of Lusaka. Mkushi massacre was the most callous in the history of the struggle as the Rhodesian army cowards slaughtered defenceless women. Most women drowned and perished in the Mkushi River trying to escape the bombing.

Mkushi was located in the middle of the bushes, thus the Rhodesian forces camped and surrounded it for about a week to make sure that it was left in ruins.

The casualties at Mkushi outnumbered those at FC camp by far. After the operation ended, we had to go to the two camps to bury our comrades and give them dignity. My cousin Lubaka, Basekulu's first born daughter perished at Mkushi. Had there been anything I could do to protect her, I would have. My other cousin Langa was lucky to escape unharmed. After the bombings, the Southern Rhodesian soldiers patrolled the camp to finish off survivors. Langa lay amongst the dead bodies, in blood bath and faked death. One must imagine how she held her breath and lay motionless until the enemy was out of sight.

When we arrived, vultures, jackals and foxes were already feasting on the bodies. It was a sorry sight. Dismembered body parts were scattered all over the place. Some deceased had their stomachs cruelly ripped open. Some bodies were already decomposing and all we could do was to shovel them off to the mass grave using tractors. The most haunting part was the lingering foul odour of decomposing bodies. That smell of human flesh is still unforgettable to date. Close to fifteen mass graves were used at Mkushi while about five were used at FC. The deceased's families never saw their resting place to pay their last respects.

Hundreds of Zambian civilians also perished in these two massacres and this angered the Zambian government whose determination to assist the freedom fighters grew. At that point, our willpower to destroy the Rhodesian army became unparalleled; we could not wait to be deployed into the country.

News soon travelled that the Dakota we shot had Green Leader, the most tactful leader of the Rhodesian army. Rumour had it that Green Leader had fought for Britain in the World War 2 where he attained his military prowess. We had heard a lot about his military tactics, which included disguising the enemy, and surprisingly we fell victim. News of his death was music to our ears and a cause for celebration to any freedom fighter including those fighting in the ZANU wing. I later learnt that the rumour of the tactical mastermind's death was after all unfounded. Green Leader died in 2016, in the present day Zimbabwe.

After the FC and Mkushi operation, a platoon was sent across Zambezi into Southern Rhodesia to burn the Rhodesian army's fuel reserves as retaliation attempt. At that time, the armed struggle had heightened and there was no turning back.

CHAPTER 5

Final kicks, ceasefire and reconciliation

The armed struggle intensified in the country and several ZIPRA companies were deployed into the country at different intervals. ZIPRA forces were largely deployed in Matebeleland and Midlands regions where ZAPU had a sphere of influence. The ZANLA wing on the other hand fought at Mashonaland and Manicaland regions where ZANU dominated. Our ZIPRA company was the last to be deployed in the country. It comprised of those that had conditions such as health issues, those who had been injured at the various bombing incidents and those who had any form of frailty.

Although I was as fit as a fiddle, I was extremely dwarfed for my age. It was actually difficult to determine my age. I looked like a teenager even in my twenties. It was for this reason that I was never allocated tough responsibilities; hence remaining in Zambia for longer, even when my comrades were already deployed in the country.

A few months after the gruesome incidents, we learnt that Boma, the camp we trained at, in Angola was bombed by the Rhodesian forces and hundreds of ZIPRA forces perished there. The bombing took place on the actual day when all the freedom fighters at Boma were to be ferried from Angola to Southern Rhodesia to join the armed struggle in 1979. A convoy of Russian Craz trucks had already lined up and soldiers were doing their final preparations with a huge excitement of finally going back home when hell broke loose.

I realised how fortunate I was to have survived these incidences. The raid was apparently a last-ditch effort by the Rhodesian army to force the freedom fighters to sit at a conference table and negotiate a shared government. The freedom fighters would not take any form of negotiation; they were prepared to fight tooth and nail to earn a total government of the country.

The Boma raid was also a response to the ZIPRA forces' shooting down of two civilian aircrafts (Air Rhodesian flight 825 and Air Rhodesian flight 827). Air Rhodesia passenger flight 825 was shot in September 1978 by the ZIPRA forces. The passenger aircraft was flying from Victoria Falls to Salisbury (present day Harare) via Kariba, a tourist resort town. The aeroplane was shot with a Strela-2-missile shortly after take-off. The missile hit the aircraft's belly, damaging it and forcing it to immediately abort the trip and do an emergency landing at a cotton field in Karoi. When the aircraft hit the ground, it broke into two parts killing 38 out of a total of 52 passengers instantly. Other surviving and injured passengers were massacred on the ground by the ZIPRA forces using automatic rifles. The ZIPRA forces got the impression that they had killed everyone. Apparently, nine passengers hid in the cotton field and lived to tell the tale.

In February 1979, the ZIPRA forces received a tip off that one of the Rhodesian Army commanders was to board Air Rhodesia 827 flying from Kariba to Salisbury. With that knowledge, an ambush was set up to shoot down the aircraft. Soon after take-off, the aircraft was brought down by a Strela-2-missile, killing all passengers on board including the crewmembers. The incident became the country's deadliest aviation disaster to date. It was soon discovered that the

Southern Rhodesian commander who was the main target and his wife had missed the flight and boarded the following flight, which landed safely in Salisbury.

The idea of shooting down the Southern Rhodesian aircrafts was to strike a snake before it strikes us again. However, what we managed to do was to scotch the snake, but failed to kill it. A scotched snake is very vicious. The shooting down of these aircrafts angered the Rhodesian army and they retaliated by bombing Boma camp.

Companies were gradually deployed into the country as the armed struggle became more aggressive. Our company, comprising largely of the physically unfit and the stunted in growth, was the last to be deployed. Meanwhile, we were taken to Jason Ziyaphapha (JZ) military school in Lusaka to work as security guards. Jason Ziyaphapha Moyo was a ZIPRA commander alongside Joshua Nkomo. Moyo had died from a mysterious parcel bomb he received while in Lusaka in 1977, hence the JZ military school was named after him. The military school trained young Black ZAPU youth who had been recently recruited.

While walking in the corridors of JZ School, I met my alleged father. This time around, I was convinced that, that was the man who gave life to me. We had grown to resemble each other like match sticks. Amongst other similar features we shared, he was dwarfed and as dark as midnight as I was. There was however, no time for father-son chit-chat moments, we were both freedom fighters at that time, although we had different duties. We were both destined to do what it takes to take back our country and begin forging relations after obtaining freedom.

One of the trainees was a young boy named Thomas. Thomas was a very inquisitive fella who enjoyed our company and resented being referred to, as a student. He would sneak in and out of the school midnight. Although we reprimanded him, we somewhat treated him as a colleague and we didn't want to be mean by reporting him or issuing him punishments. Although we were lenient with him and thought of him as just a hyperactive boy, incapable of injuring a fly, Commander Mawema was always suspicious of him and thought of him as very scandalous. They therefore developed bad blood because of those suspicions.

One evening, I was awakened by a loud noise akin to that of a gunshot, but it sounded a bit further from the dorm that I shared with Thomas and few other trainees. Soon after the noise was heard, Thomas walked in and I asked him where he was coming from at midnight, and if he had heard the noise. Thomas had a solid alibi; he said he was coming from visiting his girlfriend and had not heard any noise. We both fell asleep and woke up the following day heeding to an unexpected parade summon. Something was definitely amiss. The first thing that came to mind was the potential attack by the enemy.

We were all questioned about our whereabouts the previous night, and if we had not seen anyone leave the dormitories. We all claimed to have been indoors and denied seeing anyone leave. We were not sure what had transpired and the commanders seemed to be beating about the bush and hesitant to hit the nail on the head. They started torturing the recruits, hoping one would admit sneaking out or point those who did. We were all struck with confusion and failed to guess what was happening. After about an hour, we were all lined up and taken to a nearby tent, one by one. Jesus Christ! A young boy lay there lifeless with his intestines protruding from his ripped stomach. The commander asked if I had no knowledge of anyone who had committed such a horrific act or anyone who had gone out midnight.

After seeing that inhumane deed, I couldn't cover up for Thomas, whether he was involved or not was not my problem, he was going to explain for himself. All I knew was that he went out midnight and came back soon after the shot was fired. Thomas was electrically tortured for four hours until he finally admitted killing the boy (one of his fellow trainees) by mistake. Thomas claimed that his intention was to kill Commander Mawema. He shot at the boy midnight, thinking it was Mawema. Thomas received the punishment I received when I lost my gun. He was put in the dungeon for about a month. He soon escaped, but was immediately hunted down and brought back to the dungeon. This time, the commanders cut his toes to disable him from fleeing again.

From JZ, our company was finally deployed to enter the country via Hurungwe, in Mashonaland west province, staying at an abandoned school called Magurekure. It was at this place that we encountered a clash with the Rhodesian forces head-on for the first time in the country. Apparently, the ova-ova radio that we used would pick the enemy's airwave transmission and vice-versa. The Rhodesian forces thus learnt that we were in the vicinity through these signals and planned an ambush. Through tip-offs, they found us prepared and waiting for them in hiding. Although we lost three comrades, they suffered heavy losses than we did.

Most of our radio communications came in codes, although sometimes codes would leak to the enemy. For instance, our alphabet was developed as follows:
A=Alpha
B=Bravo
C=Cairo
D=Delta

Whenever a communiqué came in letters like this, we knew that each letter represented a certain alphabet and we would piece together the alphabets to find meaning. Although such communication was used to disguise the enemy, particularly in written form, sometimes the intended recipients would miss the message especially when they were under pressure. It took time and a certain level of intelligence to piece together those alphabets. Sometimes the letters would lend in the hands of the enemy who would understand the message and retaliate or abort a planned mission.

For obvious directives such as *'shoot'*, *'take cover'*, *'stop shooting'*, or *'the enemy is advancing'*, we had codes that we used in the battlefield verbally or through the use of voice overs. For instance, the word *'mbudzi'* would mean 'stop shooting'. The biggest challenge that both the freedom fighters and the Rhodesian forces had was communication breakdown because of technological challenges, information leak and spying on each other. There seemed to be an inside-man in each wing, leaking information to the other. After the Hurungwe clash with the enemy, our company moved to Kazangarara. We would move every time after a clash with the enemy and after the enemy studied our movements. The plan was to keep our rivals off balance.

The two freedom fighters (ZIPRA and ZANLA)'s armed wings generally made tactical mistakes during the armed struggle that the enemy took advantage of. We were suspicious of each other at the height of the war, with contrasting military strategies, often fighting against each other. Each wing fought predominantly in its territorial regions. Most of our ZIPRA comrades were deployed in regions such as Plumtree, Kezi and Matebeleland at large where ZAPU dominated.

The war of liberation finally came to a halt in 1979 and the battle worn in favour of the Black majority. The official halt of the war was sealed at the London Lancaster House Conference of December 1979 where all parties involved agreed upon a cease-fire. A resolution to settle political differences was passed, and two Black Nationalist parties ZAPU and ZANU agreed to merge their two armed wings. A peacekeeping force was formed to ensure that there was no re-arming.

All soldiers, respective of which party they belonged to, were called into their assemble points in 1980. The ZIPRA forces did not understand the whole concept of the ceasefire as it wasn't very transparent. The Rhodesian peace keeping forces would ferry people to their assemble points. At that point, mistrust of Abelungu was inevitable; we were all in disbelief that the war was indeed over. ZIPRA had 7 assemble points, namely Lima in Madlambudzi, Romeo in Hurungwe, Papa in Mount Pleasant, Gwayi river mine in Nkayi, Sierra in Lower Gweru, Saint Paul in Lupane, and Silalabuhwa near Gwanda and Beitbridge. The aim of assembling freedom fighters was an attempt to integrate them into the National Army, respective of the armed wing they belonged to.

Upon integration into the National Army, most former ZIPRA army commanders felt that the integration was unfair as they were stripped off the leadership positions they previously held. Most leadership positions were given to former ZANLA cadres.

After ceasefire, I was deployed at Guinea Fowl in Gweru, and became the Corporal Section Commander. Mistrust escalated as former ZIPRA cadres mysteriously disappeared one by one. Rumour soon travelled that they were being murdered. I decided to run away before I was the next victim.

The victimisation was not only happening to former ZIPRA forces at assemble points in the predominantly ZANU dominated regions. At Entumbane assembly in Bulawayo, the former ZANLA soldiers also escaped fearing for their lives and went back to Mashonaland. Reconciliation was far from sinking in between ZIPRA and ZANLA forces. With the countrywide mysterious disappearance of ZIPRA soldiers at different assembly points, ZIPRA soldiers ran away from the assemble points and went back to the bush. Although the end of the war of liberation was an achievement at the time, a war of ethnic groups lied ahead.

CHAPTER 6

Gukurahundi, *'a moment of madness'*

. . . .

***

MOVING BACK TO MOVE FORWARD:
The country's political history

***

t was when I joined the armed struggle that I began to learn a lot about the politics of the country. At Nampundu, we were repeatedly told of how Black nationalists started opposing the Southern Rhodesian government's oppression of Black people and events that unfolded leading to the start of the armed struggle. We often sat around the glowing fires in the evenings at Nampundu and those accustomed to the politics of the country would share stories of how Joshua Nkomo was the biblical Moses of Black Southern Rhodesians leading them to the promised land.

Apparently, from the 1930s, the Black natives began to oppose colonial rule in Southern Rhodesia. They got tired of being stripped of their fertile lands and reduced to Abelungu' servants in farms and mines. In 1957, Umdala, Joshua Nkomo formed the Southern Rhodesia African National Congress

(SRANC), later called African National Congress (ANC) in Bulawayo as the first anti-colonialist government party. The party opposed the oppression and discriminatory laws against Black people at the time. The party became a threat to the Rhodesian government, as a result, it was banned in 1959 and its leaders and followers arrested. At the time of arrest, Nkomo was out of the country; hence, he circumstantially dodged the arrest. Umdala's ancestors must have been at work, narrowly saving him from arrest, I soliloquised.

The following year, the ANC is said to have resurfaced as the National Democratic Party (NDP) with Joshua Nkomo still maintaining the President position. The NDP became popular amongst the Black educated people across the country who joined and supported it. In 1961, the NDP was banned and Nkomo founded the Zimbabwe African Peoples' Union (ZAPU). Umdala must have been as stubborn as a mule. I thought. Would I have done the same in his shoes? Absolutely not. I don't have such patience.

In 1963, party members such as Ndabaningi Sithole and Herbert Chitepo and other members broke out of ZAPU to form the Zimbabwe African National Union (ZANU) dissatisfied with Nkomo's military tactics. ZAPU's armed wing became the Zimbabwe People's Revolutionary Army (ZIPRA) while ZANU's was termed the Zimbabwe African National Liberation Army (ZANLA). It was at this point that the two parties drew their support from the country's dominant ethnic groups. ZAPU attained a predominantly Ndebele following while ZANU attained a Shona following.

The tale was beginning to make sense. This explained the toxic ethnic divide in the country. I supposed. One of the frequently asked questions whenever the political history of the country arose was Nkomo's identity. Was he Ndebele or was he Kalanga?

Apparently, Joshua Nkomo was Sotho by origin and Kalanga by naturalization. His identity has forever been a bone of contention in the country. Although world widely known as Ndebele for political influence purposes, his forefathers were the Sotho from South Africa. Although Nkomo was Sotho by origin, his family attained their Kalanga identity by naturalization when they arrived in Zimbabwe. Nkomo could easily fit into any identity in Zimbabwe, among the Ndebele, he became a Ndebele and among the Kalanga, he was Kalanga, hence his mistaken identity (*Nkomo a naturalized Kalanga: History expert*. Newsday 06-05-2015).

The tales made more sense, especially when we began witnessing the armed struggle as it happened. Apparently, some of the ZAPU freedom fighters who were parcel bombed or died mysteriously were not killed by Abelungu, but by ZANU freedom fighters to settle political scores and personal beefs. The series of questions we had, often interfered with the chronology of these tales, nonetheless, no stone was left unturned. We were as inquisitive as lower primary grade learners.

It was thus tribal tension between ZANU and ZAPU that pioneered the start of a long history of tribal conflict unlikely to end even centuries after the country's independence. After the split in 1963, the parties were suspicious of each other although each of them remained committed to the armed struggle fighting a common enemy, the Rhodesian Front (RF), the settlers' party.

In 1964, Ian Smith became the country's Prime Minister and persuaded the British government to grant independence of the white minority in Southern Rhodesia. In 1965, Ian Smith pronounced the Unilaterally Declared Independence (UDI) under white settler minority rule and this outraged the Black nationalists who decided to take action against the settlers. Other countries such as Russia and China did not recognize this declaration; hence, they were prepared to offer aid to

Black nationalists in case of war. At this point, it started making sense why the Russians were training us.

The settlers' suppression of Black political activities, police brutality and the exploitation of Black labour left Black political leaders like Joshua Nkomo with no option but to respond with violence by sending young men and women to neighbouring countries such as Angola and Zambia to train for guerrilla warfare. The Ian Smith government anticipated the arming of Black nationalists and sent military observers to countries like Malaysia, Kenya and Vietnam to study the guerrilla warfare that was to be used by Black nationalists. The two armies, ZANLA and ZIPRA were suspicious of each other at the height of the war. We had contrasting military strategies and often fought against each other when we clashed.

When we (the Black majority) won the armed struggle in 1979, national elections were held in 1980 and these gave ZANU the majority seats in Parliament resulting in Robert Mugabe, the ZANU leader proclaimed as the Prime Minister. We failed to understand why Mugabe would be the Prime Minister when it was Nkomo who pioneered the armed struggle. As far as we knew, ZAPU played a major role in the armed struggle.

After 1980, mistrust between the two-armed wings, ZANLA and ZIPRA continued and worsened, with the Prime Minister accusing us (ZIPRA forces) of not surrendering the armed struggle weapons in a bid to later overthrow the government. We could not surrender all our weapons when the reconciliation process was not transparent. Everything was happening fast and suspicions were inevitable.

A series of fights broke up between our armed wings (ZIPRA and ZANLA) with fights lasting a few days. We (ZIPRA forces) were reluctant to join the newly integrated army due to mysterious disappearances of those who did. ZANU suspicions of ZAPU led them to charge ZAPU leaders Lookout

Masuku, Dumiso Dabengwa and others with treason and later detaining them. Seeing these terrifying events, Joshua Nkomo feared for his life and fled into exile to the United Kingdom. The absence of our ZAPU leaders forced most of us (ex ZIPRA fighters) to flee the national army in fear for our lives.

Meanwhile, Robert Mugabe assigned North Koreans to train a militia from the ZANLA forces called the fifth brigade in 1980 that was to be sent to Matebeleland and Midlands, Nkomo's areas of influence to restore order and uproot unwanted weeds. The fifth brigade was sanctioned to massacre our strongholds in Matebeleland and destroy us (ex-combatants) commonly framed as dissidents.

I later learnt that the actual aim of the massacre was to liquidate Joshua Nkomo's political influence and destroy our ZAPU party. The operation was termed *Gukurahundi,* (a term that means to remove unwanted weeds) by the ZANU Government; it is world widely known as the Matebeleland genocide. Ever since the Gukurahundi massacres, attempts to reconcile Zimbabwean ethnic groups have been in vain. Although many ethnic groups were affected by the genocide, the Ndebele and the Kalanga were the most affected as they constituted the majority of people living in rural Matebeleland region where the genocide was mostly intense.

Approximately between 20 000 to 30 000 people were killed, others displaced in this ethnic cleansing between 1982 and 1987. The number of deaths alone can never quantify the damage caused by terror; displacements were also major. Our comrades fled and dispersed to different regions such as Bulawayo, Botswana and South Africa. These displacements marked the beginning of a huge exodus, the Zimbabwe diaspora migration.

Gukurahundi finally halted in 1987, seven years after the Lancaster House Conference, which was a peace negotiation session. Robert Mugabe later called the Gukurahundi '*a mo-*

ment of madness' and signed a Unity Accord on 22 December 1987 (representing ZANU) with Joshua Nkomo (representing ZAPU). Robert Mugabe who had been the Country's Prime Minister became the official President of Zimbabwe and Joshua Nkomo became the Vice President and the Unity Accord resulted in a newly formed reconciliation party called Zimbabwe African National Union-Patriotic Front (ZANU-PF).

As ZAPU followers, predominantly Ndebele and Kalanga speaking people who had been largely affected by the Gukurahundi, we felt that Joshua Nkomo had sold us out by signing the Unity Accord. The Unity Accord did not benefit ZAPU, even the name of the reconciliation party retained Mugabe's party' identity. No efforts were made to redress the Gukurahundi crimes or account for the political decision to launch it, up to the present day.

The reconciliatory rhetoric after the armed struggle was at this point far-fetched. I was one of those who fled from the national army during the reconciliation process when I felt that my life was in danger. In 1982, I decided to go home when Gukurahundi started, but I knew very well that my life was in danger. All ZIPRA soldiers who ran away from the army became fugitives.

CHAPTER 7

Back to school

boarded a train from Bulawayo to Plumtree, kuTitshi. Titshi loosely translates to 'station'. Plumtree is known as kuTitshi because the city has a huge train station where trains from Botswana, Bulawayo and Hwange stop and exchange passengers and freight. Everyone in the train was minding their own business. I failed to ignore the rattling sound coming from below the train. Metals seemed to be rasping against each other, causing a vibration sound on my teeth. I looked outside the window the entire journey reflecting about my life and simultaneously trying to diagram my future. I recalled the near death experiences I had almost succumbed to. I felt lucky to be alive.

The route between Bulawayo and kuTitshi cuts through farms growing different crops and also rearing cattle. Now that Zimbabwe was free, would chocolate-skinned men ever own such fertile lands and farms? How would the redistribution of land take place? Would there ever be peace between ZAPU and ZANU members? Would the Ndebele and the Shona ever co-exist peacefully in the country? Before I knew it, the train blew its horn signalling its arrival kuTitshi.

It was around 12 midday when I jumped off the train. I had to rush to board a bus that connects to the village. As far as I remembered, there was only one bus using the kuTitshi-Masendu route. Its departure time was always between 12:00 and 13:00. By that time, the villagers who would have come to the city for shopping would be anticipated to have completed all their errands. I ran to the bus terminus, lucky enough, the bus was still there. The bus conductors were busy loading and tying up luggage on the deck of the bus roof. The driver was selling bus tickets. His face had grown purple and pale by calling the names of all the villages that the bus was going to pass by and stop at: *Thekwane, Council, Maplanka, Tokwana, Nopemano, Masendu, Nyabane, Luvuluma, Khame, Ndolwane and Makhulela.* He had to make sure that passengers boarded the right bus.

I joined the queue, paid for my ticket and placed my luggage on the seat, this was and still is the simplest way to communicate that the seat is reserved. I went out of the bus to buy snacks for the road. I loved my cream buns and coca-cola. I had not eaten since morning. After the ticket selling session, the driver started the bus engine. Even today you will find those passengers who only get into the bus when the driver starts the engine or when the bus is in motion, I was one of them. I extinguished my cigarette and fought my way into the already overloaded bus. At least I had reserved my seat, so I went straight to my seat. Other passengers were standing on the aisle, holding onto the metal poles that stood tall behind each and every seat. I suppose they were designed for overload moments such as those.

At exactly 12:45, the bus was set in motion with more than 20 standing passengers. Conductors had no space in the bus; they climbed onto its roof. As soon as the bus took off, passengers began digging into varieties of foods stretching from buns, biscuits, mealies, fresh chips, lunchboxes of pap, samp to things I can't even describe. The awful smell of those different kinds of foods polluted the bus for a while. Even the open bus windows could not ventilate the stench and refresh the overloaded sweaty passengers. Passengers dropped off at different bus stops and after some time, most of them stopped eating. The smell finally subsided after an hour and as other passengers dropped off, others got seats, relieving those standing.

One old man who drank beer the entire journey refused to take a seat even though vacant seats availed as people dropped off. He was so drunk that we feared he would miss his drop off point. He started chanting songs of the struggle and narrating tales of how Ian Smith's Rhodesian army was defeated. Although drunk, his voice was so commanding that it drew everyone's attention. While some of his utterances were fabrications, we all listened. He spiced his talk with an element of humour such that we would burst with laughter now and then. He described how the enemy's aeroplane was taken down in Zambia as if he was there. He dramatized how it was ripped apart and fell to the ground. He was a storyteller, though a little bit spiced, he definitely told the story better than I would have.

Although I felt the urge to zero in and correct him about how the events actually unfolded, it was too dangerous to publicly speak about such issues, particularly when the Gukurahundi terror had just begun. I could never know who was in that bus, I had to tread carefully. Such talks could only be left to alcoholics and lunatics who often get away with saying anything anywhere. In between his story telling, he would chant the song;

Sakhala, sakhal'isibhamu
Isibhamu, eZimbabwe
eZimbabwe
Yena USmith wayivum'imajority

The witty old man made my journey seem shorter than it was. I occasionally joined in, silently singing along in my mind. I could not publicly join Mr Wit's chants, I was sane, but deep down in my heart of hearts, I was as insane as he was.

Upon arriving home 6 years later, so much had changed; the village looked like an abandoned warzone. Roads had been ripped by landmine blasts. Plumtree was one of the entrance ports for trained ZIPRA soldiers from the neighbouring country. Thus, the Rhodesian soldiers used undercover explosives in their tactics, they would plant landmines to destroy ZIPRA vehicles transporting soldiers into the country. Several homes had been torched, particularly those where Black soldiers would seek refuge, ask for food or had girlfriends in. A Black man was tormented for being in solidarity with a fellow Black man.

The once close-knit village had become an enemy to itself. Neighbours were forced to become spies of their own people. Death threats were common to those who refused to comply. The Rhodesian army recruited Black puppet soldiers that they used as informants when penetrating villages. Most villagers, mostly elderly people, mistook every Black man for a nationalist fighting against the Rhodesian forces. The disguise caused a lot of confusion and left a lot of people dead.

The village was now largely dominated by elderly men, women and children. All physically fit and young people had either willingly joined the armed struggle or were abducted to join. The sad part was that most of these people had perished at FC, Mkushi and Boma bombing massacres yet others died during the actual war. Their relatives anticipated their comeback but in vain. They could not even set foot where they lay.

A cloud of lifelessness covered the village. Trees and grass seemed to have been deadened by this war. Even people who remained behind appeared emotionally and psychologically drained. Both the earth and its inhabitants appeared to be reflecting the horrors of the war. A form of spiritual cleansing and restoration would perhaps breathe life to the desolate environment that was once the only heaven we knew.

The trip from the bus stop where I dropped off seemed longer than expected. A lot was going on in my mind. I was also trying to ignore the cramp on my butt for sitting too long in the bus. Along the way, I saw familiar faces; people who seemed to recognise me. None of us uttered any greetings. I believed that in the years I had spent in the bush, I had changed physically. I joined the struggle as a teenage boy and came back as a grown man. I was a fugitive; I didn't want my whereabouts to be known because sooner or later, I would be pursued. Thus, I could not afford any chit-chat greetings with anyone. I suppose they also could not greet me based on my position. Soldiers are unpredictably brutal, one would not want to mistakenly step on their corns verbally.

I arrived home around 4pm. There seemed to be no one to welcome me. All the huts were locked except the kitchen. Kitchen rondavels were rarely locked in villages. This allowed un-announced visitors to rest in, drink water when thirsty or even prepare tea for themselves. Back in the day, communication was not a thumb away or a dial away as today, most visitors came unannounced, as there was no way of announcing visits. There were no telephones in the villages, so visitors would visit anytime they felt like.

I was that visitor. I went straight to the kitchen and helped myself with leftovers. Gogo had prepared millet stiff pap with amasi (sour creamed milk). Good Lord! I had not eaten that meal in ages. I quickly munched and munched without hesitation; it was Gogo's kitchen after all. I could not wait to be served. I was finally home. As soon as my tummy was full, I took Gogo's reed-made mat, spread it on the floor and rested. Millet pap is very heavy in the stomach such that one cannot help but nap afterwards especially after not eating it for quite some time.

I am not sure for how long I slept but I was awoken by sounds of goats bleating for their young ones that were weaned into the garden in the morning to keep them away from forest jackals who prey on the little ones who cannot run as much in times of danger. A few minutes later, I heard Gogo calling her goats by name and opening the garden for the young ones to join their mothers. A minute later, she opened the gate and I heard her lamenting about the huge footprints that had gone towards the direction of the kitchen. She was complaining about people who walk into people's houses stealing meal-ie-meal and other household essentials. I lay there still and decided to surprise her as she opened the door.

As soon as she opened the door and caught sight of me laying on my stomach and covering my face, she made a deafening scream, half spilling the bucket of water she was carrying on her head. I immediately stood up to assure her that it wasn't a stranger, it was me, her grandson. It took her about three minutes to recover from the shock and she started breathing normally.

I learnt never to prank elderly people. After recovering from the shock, she welcomed me with a theatrical kind of joy, dramatically embracing me, articulating praise names, thanking the ancestors for keeping me safe and weeping at the same time. I did not know what to take of what was hap-pening; I just felt good being in Gogo's arms. The thunderous scream that she had made upon seeing me had automatically invited neighbours who came running and storming into the yard, carrying knobkerries and spears to check on what befell Gogo. Some neighbours still had the humanity to look out for neighbours.

Although the neighbours were happy to see me, I did not need the kind of attention they were awarding me. Had Gogo not screamed, I was going to stay undercover in the village until I could concoct my next move. Other than being a fugitive, I wasn't prepared to answer questions from my neighbours who were keen to ask about their children. I could not afford to be the bearer of sad news.

Gogo looked frail. I wasn't sure if it was a result of ageing or she was unwell. Her being her, she claimed that she was as healthy as a horse. I helped Gogo rekindle the fire while she tidied the kitchen and swept the kitchen front. She was extremely inquisitive about what transpired from the moment I left the country in 1976 to date. I honestly had no energy to tell the long tale. Besides, I was not prepared to be taken aback to the trauma I went through. I had not yet healed enough to reminisce or to share my experiences. I however alerted Gogo that I had run away from the National army. I was away without official leave, AWOL according to the army language. I was a wanted fugitive according to the army laws, so I planned to lay low and stay undercover in order to save myself from being abducted and killed.

I asked Gogo about mother and everybody else in the family. I learnt that mother had five other children with her husband that I did not know about. I had three sisters and two brothers in Chivhu where she was married. I wondered how they looked like, if they even knew about me. Sometimes when women get married, they don't disclose about the children they had out of wedlock. When mother got married, I didn't remember any sort of introductions being made to the in-laws that I was her child. Perhaps I was too young to take cognisance of such details. Gogo prepared a bed for me in the other hut and we both retired to bed.

The next moment I was conscious of myself, I saw the man I believed was my father wearing soiled and torn clothes. He was roaming about the village aimlessly like a mentally disturbed delusional person. He would dance and sing, attracting passer-bys and entertaining onlookers. Bystanders seemed startled about what befell the well-known and respected teacher. I was amongst the onlookers but he did not notice my presence. He seemed to confess to the growing audience that he had thrown his own first-born child into the river and he was asking for assistance in rescuing him before he drowns. What followed was a sudden mayhem of a swarm of bees stinging people and screams were heard all over the area. Before we knew it, a sudden downpour of rain akin to the Biblical Noah's floods started and I ran, taking shelter under the nearby Mopane tree, which stood tall, dwarfing other trees like the Biblical Goliath.

As the rainfall intensified, the Mopane tree became useless; it let loose the now heavy droplets of water that had initially camped on the tree leaves before the rain intensified. While trying to concoct plan B of escape, suddenly the sound of a bellowing bull sent shivers down my spine, and as if electrocuted, I sprang up from the slumber. It was the sound of a bellowing bull outside the yard. Thank God, it was a dream.

I woke up to a glowing fire in Gogo's thatched kitchen. As a traditional man, it was taboo to report to the kitchen in the morning before reporting to the kraal. A kraal was associated with manhood; it was the epitome of men's wealth. Even when men died in the village, they were buried behind the kraal while women were buried behind the kitchen or the granary where they stored their harvests. Women were defined by the size of their granaries while men were defined by the number of livestock they had.

The sight of cows and goats rubbing and embracing each other lovingly was heart-warming. The aromatic scent of cow-dung was the official sweet morning greeting that I had missed. That morning I felt nature spoke to me, 'Welcome home, this is your village'.

A few minutes later, I was wolfing on Gogo's inviting breakfast and catching up on the news of everything that transpired in my absence. Although ageing, Gogo's memory was as sharp as tack. She could recall and detail things that happened many years ago. While at it, I began recalling the dream I had, particularly the first part when my father was seeking help in rescuing his firstborn son. The other parts of the dream were too disjointed to puzzle together, I decided to ignore them.

Although I was sceptical, I began sharing my dream with Gogo. She was always the kind that usually interrupts when one is speaking by asking questions midway or making facial gestures but for a first, she was too quiet as if she was being extremely careful of what to and what not to say. Issues of absent fathers have a bearing on children's lives. One ought to be careful when such talks arise.

The issue surrounding my paternal family had never been discussed as far as I remember. If it was, it was done in my absence. Although I could not see any sense of emotion from Gogo's face after sharing my dream, I knew that grandmothers always knew the truth about who our real fathers were. She did not comment about the dream. This is unlike grandmothers. According to them, there is no dream without a meaning. There was certainly something she was shying away from, and not telling. I looked straight into her eyeballs and asked her if the man was my father. Had I given her a chance, she would have dodged the question, but she could not.

As far as she knew, he was my father and I resembled him and his people. I decided to confront this omission in my life. I recalled my meeting with him at JZ in Lusaka. Although there was not much time for chatting, we related as father and son, more than as mere teacher and former student. Awkward! Wasn't it? Maybe I was delusional and seeing wrong signals but we had this different connection, something that had been missing all my life.

I was not sure if he had yet returned from JZ and made it alive into the country. However, everyone was called into the country in 1980 for reconciliation purposes and he was too old to join the army, hence I was hopeful that he returned home safe and sound. I was sceptical and nervous about this confrontation but I decided not to allow my nerves to short circuit my brain. I needed to know the truth and I needed closure.

I spent most of my time indoors, operating incognito, trying to keep my arrival unannounced to the entire village. The few villagers that had seen me, spread the news and I soon had visitors who came with live chickens as welcome back gifts. I could tell that people had questions, but no one was brave enough to ask any. I wore a straight-face and never gave anyone a chance. I was not mentally and psychologically ready to share my experiences.

Days following the dream, I was stuck in a binary thinking about confronting my father. One voice saying I should, and the other saying I should not. After a week, I felt that I was bold enough to face my alleged father and or his people, depending on availability. I left home when the urge of confrontation was still fresh and walked as fast as I could before my nerves got the best of me. I arrived at his homestead around 15.00 and my alleged father was fencing the goats' kraal using evenly cut thin poles. As soon as he saw me, his energy seemed to diminish. Although he had a strong-willed character, there was something vulnerable and tender in his strength.

At least we did not have to get into the homestead, we spoke as real men do, chewing all their matters by the kraal. I wasn't sure of what words to use in this confrontation and I do not remember what I said to him. The next minute he stopped what he was doing and invited me to sit on the long log lying next to the kraal. He called his two brothers who had just arrived from a hunting expedition. After exchanging greetings with the brothers, my alleged father informed them that I was his firstborn son whom he bore when he was still young, unprepared and uneasy about raising a child. In my mind, I was wondering why this man would address his brothers instead of talking to me. I had confronted him and I was the centre of all this, but he spoke as if I was invisible. I felt useless like a refuse can. It's the little things that sting the most.

I gathered my guts and questioned him why he did not come for me if he knew that I was his son. What he thought I was eating? Whom he thought paid my school fees and bought uniforms? We lived in the same village, he taught me in class, and he occasionally sent me home to fetch school fees, which Gogo did not have in many instances. He watched me drop out of school and still did nothing. He knew too well that I did not live with mother, hence I was deprived of the ideal parenthood that every child should have. His explanations were as shallow as ankle deep. I was angry, but for progress sake, I decided to let bygones be bygones and iron out my differences with my father. I was now a grown man; I would in the long run need his blessings when it came to marriage or starting a family.

After the dramatic confrontation, one of the brothers decided that we go home and meet the broader family, including his children and wife. Apparently, everyone knew about my existence. The talk that my father had with his brothers outside was just a formality one; otherwise, I was seemingly not a stranger to their ears. I was introduced to my siblings and I tried to search myself in their eyes. I could neither locate myself nor read their thoughts about me. Although I had mixed emotions about the unfolding of this identity, I was as identical as matchsticks with my people.

After this visit, I occasionally visited my father seeking for advice on what I should do with my life. He suggested that I go back to school and start over my life. In the new dispensation, it was the educated ones who would live graceful lives. He suggested that I enrol for school at a different village altogether so that my identity is not traceable since I was a fugitive and Gukurahundi was looming faster than wildfire.

I pondered on the issue of going to school. I was honestly too old for that. Staying at home was dangerous. It was inevitable that sooner or later, the ZANU soldiers would locate me. I asked Gogo for my birth certificate which she always kept. To my surprise she could not find it, she suspected that it may have been amongst the papers that she burnt thinking that they were useless documents.

Schools were not like the army; one could not enrol without a birth certificate. I had to manoeuvre my way, applying for one at old age. The loss of my birth certificate was a blessing in disguise. This time around, I had the chance of deciding my own name. I used one of my army names. On my new birth certificate, I became Freedom Dube. Black and Mambazo were reduced to nick names.

I took heed of my father's advice of going back to school and enrolled at Gonde Primary School incognito, staying with one of my neighbours who was a teacher there. At least I was not known in that area, so it was a safe space to stay undercover. Only a few teachers knew my secret. It was a time when people were unselfish; everyone understood the plight of the other, hence selling out was not common especially amongst the educated. I was 23 years of age and my looks did not sell me either. I was very short and fit in the school uniform like a glove. I blended into the school like a chameleon because of my demeanour. I had a tiny body and very short in height and I also occasionally behaved like a child.

During the liberation war, schools were closed and not functional for about five years. So, when they eventually opened, every child enrolled for the grade or form that they had left off from. Bear in mind that at the time children enrolled for grade one late. Years did not matter at the time. Entrance was not determined by the age of a child; it was determined by the child's ability to cross their right hand above the head and touch the left ear. If they could not reach out to touch the ear, they stayed at home until they could try again the following year. So imagine how old the grade 5 learners were in the post-war period.

Although I fit perfectly into the school system, I related well with teachers more than with fellow students. I drank beer, shared cigars with teachers and the headmaster after school, and occasionally chilled with them in the staffroom. I was mature and understood life the way they did. I could sense that fellow students did not fathom my relationship with teachers.

At the time, under normal circumstances, one could not easily relate with teachers. Learners had to think about what to say when they met a teacher. Teachers were highly respected and feared. Whenever learners randomly met a teacher during weekends, they would make a U-turn and avoid any sort of contact. What escalated the fear was the thought of greeting the teacher in English. Although we learnt English at school, the language remained foreign, whenever one tried to imitate the teacher, the tongue would fail one. Learners would relieve themselves in class as they failed to imitate what the teacher taught them to say when nature called. "Please teacher, may I go to the toilet", was the correct statement. Some would not empty their bowels until the end of class in fear of speaking in English. Those who were brave enough would just chew the Queen's language and mumble it. "Please teacher may I go di toilet".

I was very intelligent even from my early years of schooling and very athletic. I played soccer and I was a sprinter, running short distances and relay. I resented the idea of competing with kids on the running track, so I would sprint, and stop midway just to prove a point. I was not one of them and I would never be one. Other learners expected teachers to issue me a punishment for my uncooperative behaviour, but that never happened.

While I was a learner there, I occasionally saw a girl whose smile haunted me every night. I was a fugitive and did not want any form of a relationship whatsoever lest I lost my tongue unaware and said things I was not supposed to say. Phela love can make you speak in tongues and confess anything. I suppressed my feelings for this girl for months. She played netball, so one day we were on a school trip, walking to our neighbour and sister school, Muke Primary, when I met her face to face with no distraction whatsoever. Her smile lit my life like a candle. That day I could not hold my guts.

She swung her tiny and narrow waist, tightly belted by her green uniform with the rhythm of the wind like a pendulum. Her beauty protruded through the school uniform. I was absolutely taken by her majestic figure. I finally gathered my guts and looked into her face. She looked very placid and wore smiling eyes. While I was stealing her, she abruptly stopped and looked at me with fixed eyes. "*Sakubona bhuti*", she extended her greetings. The way she parted her lips and stared at me made me realise that the girl had accumulated power over me, she could boil or freeze my blood with one stare and glance of her eyes.

Her twins stood firm from her chest as if they were made of mortar. I loved her to the point of distraction. Loved or lusted? Not sure but either of the two. All I did was to imagine myself on her bosoms. When she greeted me, I momentarily froze as words evicted themselves from my tongue. I finally said "*Wamuhle ntokazi*", I wasn't responding to her, I was articulating what I was seeing. She was a gem of creation. She responded shyly and said, "*Ngyabonga*". We exchanged few words. Her name was Benkosi Moyo. A beautiful name it is.

I would not tell you how I played my cards, but I proposed love right away. That was the right opportunity as we had to walk about 6 miles before reaching our destination. She could not dodge me. I tried every trick, but seemingly could not break the loin walls surrounding her heart. She dismissed my mores so candidly. Maybe she needed time, girls back in the day never declared love on their first wooing encounter.

She however seemed inquisitive about me, who I was, where I originally came from, why I chilled with teachers after school, how old I was, blah blah blah. One thing I hated about women was their inquisitiveness. I felt I was losing myself in the process. At our guerrilla trainings, we were never taught to be this soft, I was a dissident. I was not supposed to beg a woman for love. Dissidents and soldiers got everything they wanted by force, but something was just different about her. She was that woman who was to bring moisture to my barren days. I had to search for my long-gone patience and surrender it to this beautiful soul. I loved her to the point of distraction.

From the series of questions, I got the impression that she already knew my name. I also sensed that I was a topic of discussion somewhere; she was in fact asking these questions on behalf of a group of other girls. Therefore, I had to be diplomatic about my responses. After the cat and mouse talk, Benkosi diplomatically refused my request. She put it candidly that she would never date Kalanga men, she only dates Ndebele men. Although I felt a sense of failure in my male guts, I made peace with the fact that this episode was perhaps just the foundation; a better structure was yet to be built. Maybe the tribal statement was just a temporal way of diplomatically dodging my request. But how could any woman reject my maleness?

I had a confrontation with myself at night, recalling my conversation with Benkoe (her shortened name). One thing I was certain about, was that she was not totally dismissive of my advances. She was willing to know more about me. That was a good sign. Wasn't it? When girls do not want anything to do with you, you feel stung by their rejection right away. I had made suggestive statements to award her time to think about me.

Apart from her beauty, she had a wifely etiquette and naturally drew respect. She also had lexical powers that challenged my own verbose. I was obviously not her match. How then was I to convince her? I had to conceive a plan on how I would ice-break the next episode.

Days and weeks passed, before I could see her. Time was moving fast and I knew that a lot of boys were stampeding over her, so I had to make a move. I had to strategically wait for her by the school's backyard gate she used when going home. The gate was a stile structure made of horizontally laid thick wood where learners climbed over as they entered or exited the school. The gate would not be opened; it was only used by learners whose home direction faced that way. The traditional structure was created to prevent goats and cattle from entering the school premises. Only animals that had a skill of climbing like baboons and monkeys could cross over the gate.

Boys being boys enjoyed sitting at the rock bottom of the gate looking up girls' uniforms as they climbed up the gate. I was too mature for that nonsense. I just wanted to talk to Benkoe wami. I felt it strongly in my bones that she was the missing rib in my life. She looked a bit timid that day, the confidence she had the last time we met seemed to have diminished. Maybe she was also nervous about meeting me. After a series of back and forth word exchange, she said, "promise you will never break my heart." From that very moment, I knew that she was mine. She must have thought about this for a while, she must have prayed that I don't disappear forever. Our relationship was an answered prayer for each of us.

I completed grade seven in 1984 and enrolled for Form 1 at Madlambudzi Secondary School in 1985. By the time I completed Grade 7, my girlfriend was pregnant. In those days, in relationships, we never spoke about sex or let me say the sex topic never arose although I suppose partners thought about it or imagined it. The topic was just a taboo. The danger of not addressing sex issues resulted in unwanted pregnancies or general lack of communication about sexual preferences. On our very first sexual encounter, I asked Benkoe if she shared a hut with anyone, if not, I was going to visit her that night. Her response was that she slept alone. From that conversation, a sex deal was automatically sealed. I knew what was to happen and I suppose she knew too. However, important details such as contraception were never discussed; I assumed that women at that stage stayed prepared for such encounters. From that day onwards, I occasionally visited her and we did the deed. Months went by, on the third month after our first intimate encounter, she told me that she was pregnant.

I did not know how to react. My response was the meanest that I would forever regret as long as I live. I told her to tell her other boyfriends. I was aware that I was the only man in her life and I had met her a virgin. We talked about such topics with other boys. It was a guy-code to never admit impregnating a girl until the child is born, when you are able to check any resemblance, calculate and match the conception period vis-à-vis the intimacy period. I can imagine what she was going through, being lambasted by her family for conceiving a fatherless child at a young age.

When a woman falls pregnant out of wedlock, there are firm traditional procedures to adhere to such as *ukubika isisu* (reporting pregnancy) to the father-to-be's family. Whether I admitted impregnating her or not, my family could not dodge this confrontation.

Her family struggled to locate my family because I was in hiding and a dissident, I had never disclosed my identity to my girlfriend. She did not know where I originally came from and she did not know my real name, the one that I was given at birth. I ignored the topic every time it arose. Therefore, her attempts to trace my family reached a dead end until she eventually confronted the teacher I stayed with at Gonde Primary School. Mr Sibanda was an elderly person who understood such circumstances; hence, he decided to disclose my identity for the sake of the child and sympathized with my girlfriend whom he knew.

Surprisingly, she and her family representatives arrived when I was home one weekend. They seemingly had strategized not to ask if I was the father-to-be, but to already declare me as one. I vividly remember one of her uncles saying, '*Asizanga kuzokulwa. Inkunzi yenu ifohlele esibayeni sethu kwawonakala*'. In the lack of a better interpretation, this translates to 'your son has wronged us'. My uncles asked me if I knew her and I denied knowing her. In the elderly people's language, knowing a girl went beyond its literal meaning, it meant being intimate with her at some point. My denial in front of her uncles and aunties I suppose destroyed her to the core. She sobbed bitterly facedown. She could not even confront me about our sexual encounters in front of the elders. She sat on the canvas mat defeated and looking numb.

Deep in my heart of hearts, I felt pity for her, she was still as beautiful as I met her and I still wanted her. But a man does not agree to every pregnancy smeared to him on the streets, lest he becomes the father of the nation. Before they left, I asked that we wait for the child to be born to check any resemblance. I guess that was an automatic admission that I knew her.

I never spoke to her or saw her until she gave birth. Meanwhile, I dated another girl whom I had neither connection with nor feelings for. I was pushing time to get myself to forget about my soon-to-be fatherhood. As boys commonly did, I asked my new girlfriend if I could come over at night and she agreed. She shared her hut with her younger sister, but nonetheless we slept together. I got a sense that this was not new to them, each one of them would bring boys in and they were both comfortable with the setup.

On my second visit, I got to the sisters' hut and went straight to my girlfriend's bed. Before we could do anything, another man whistled from outside. To my astonishment, my girlfriend dressed up and left me in bed. Jesus Christ! I failed to understand what had just happened. This woman had just insulted my manhood. I failed to come to terms with this embarrassment; I decided to roll over to the sister's bed. She welcomed me and warmed my cold self into sleep. I guess sisters stood in the gap for each other.

I woke up around 3am to go back home before I could be caught. As soon as I exited the yard, a giant owl ferociously attacked me. I never knew witchcraft existed until that day. I tried to cover my head using my jacket, but I would feel the owl's claws clasping my head and ears. It would let go of me, fly around and come back to scratch my head again. I would feel its heavy weight as it landed on my head. I would take cover whenever it approached but in vain. I ran for my life, but the huge bird wouldn't let go of me. The owl attacked me for about a mile and disappeared into thin air after a while. That was the last day I visited that girl and I never told the story to anyone until about 10 years later. I lied about the scratches on my head until they healed. The story was outrageous and unbelievable even after so many years.

A month after Benkoe gave birth, she brought the baby home. The first thing that Gogo did when she was handed the baby was to lift the blanket that wrapped her and stared at her feet. She looked at me and said, 'Grandson, this is your daughter. These are our feet'. From then onwards, I assumed the fatherly responsibilities. Gogo had performed her DNA tests by just looking at the baby's feet. Who was I to challenge her?

My family sent representatives to pay *inhlawulo* (damages). By paying the damages, we were acknowledging as a family that the child is ours; she belonged to the Dube clan. We did not have much to support the child. Gogo occasionally sold sugar beans and goats so that she buys clothes for the baby. I knew I had a child, but I wasn't sure of what it meant to be a father. What was I supposed to do? Mother left me with Gogo before I could pronounce the word 'mama'. Where does one learn to be a parent?

Meanwhile, the girlfriend I was messing with until the dramatic owl saga told me that she was pregnant. I had no strings attached with her, and whether the baby was mine or not, I was going to deny. I recalled the day she left me sleeping in her blankets while she left with another man. Even her sister could witness that as she solaced me in her blankets. What if the sister was pregnant too? My life was a mess.

I denied responsibility and told her never to mention my name to her family as I would embarrass her in front of her people and tell them what transpired the night I went for a sleep over. The child was born resembling the other man like peas in a pod. Although I thought I had escaped a dramatic episode in my life, the rumours of me fathering the child never disappeared until a time when she approached me as a teenager to confront me about her paternity. I referred her back to her mother.

Gukurahundi deepened in Plumtree; more soldiers were deployed to sweep off ZIPRA soldiers and their relatives. The painful part is that the "ethnic cleansing" did not only target former ZIPRA soldiers, but anyone speaking Ndebele and Kalanga was a victim. Children and women were brutally killed. ZANLA soldiers often disguised villagers and pretended to be ZIPRA soldiers to determine which side villagers sympathised with. Those who seemed to sympathise with the opposition party were often beaten to death. Only villagers brave enough to differentiate the combats and tongue accent survived the disguise.

One day ZIPRA dissidents laid an ambush at Khame village. ZANLA soldiers then received a tip off, reinforced and attacked in numbers. Households that were said to be hosting the enemy were searched and dwellers tortured. One home was surrounded by ZANLA soldiers searching for the enemy. While others were in hiding, a few soldiers entered the home to ask where the dissidents were. As soon as they entered the gate, a young 12-year-old boy ran and hid himself inside a 50kg empty sack at the granary without the elders noticing. After a few word exchange between the soldiers and the household elders, the soldiers sought for permission to search the home, which they were granted. They searched all houses in the homestead and eventually searched the granary. When they got to the granary, they saw a moving object in the sack and mistakenly shot instantly, thinking it was a ZIPRA dissident in hiding.

The boy's family was devastated as they had not noticed that the boy went in hiding when he saw the soldiers. Efforts to resuscitate him were fruitless as his stomach was ripped open and his insides bulging. He departed in few minutes.

News soon travelled that I was a returned dissident and in hiding. Sell-outs sold me out and soldiers invaded our home where Gogo stayed alone. I occasionally visited about twice a month on weekends. Fortunately, I had not gone home that weekend when our home was invaded. Gogo was held hostage in her own hut and cornered to reveal where I was. To save her own life, Gogo told the soldiers that I stayed at Gonde and posed undercover as a student.

Knowing that I could be armed, and potentially dangerous, the soldiers did not set up an ambush right away. They knew that I was trained to be suspicious of activities and sniff danger from afar. They began seeking information from learners at Gonde Primary School who knew about me. Although I was still staying at Mr Sibanda's cottage, I had since graduated from Primary School and enrolled at Madlambudzi Secondary School. Gonde Primary leaners knew me as I was staying at the teacher's cottage and spent a lot of time with teachers after school. Apparently, Benkoe, although our relations had soured and she wasn't aware that I was a fugitive, she heard that soldiers were looking for me and she confronted me to enquire why I was wanted. Little did she know that she had tipped me off by that confrontation. I denied knowledge of why soldiers would want to know about me.

I began formulating an escape plan. I knew that the school was perhaps under surveillance and I was likely to be abducted midnight. I went to the house I shared with Mr Sibanda. He had gone out. I wore feminine clothes that his girlfriend had left the last time she came for a sleepover. I put on a very long skirt, tied a doek on my head and carried a 20-litre metal container on my head as women did in those days when fetching water. That is how I saved my ass from the planned ambush. From that moment onwards, I knew that my stay in the country was dangerous. I had to flee for my life.

CHAPTER 8

Egoli

· · · · · ·

took the risk and went to my village of origin overnight. I needed cash before I could leave the country. I couldn't risk sleeping at home though, I slept at a friend's place in transit to visit Gogo in the morning. Gogo was equally broke, thus, she advised that I sell goats to fundraise for my trip. I sold two goats for $8 to my neighbour Maphosa, and spent my last night at a friend's place again. The following morning, I was to leave the village heading for South Africa via Botswana. I owned neither a passport nor a visa to enter these two countries, but nothing would stop me. I was determined.

It was a cold rainy morning, when I woke up. The sky was overcast with slightly thick and grey broiling nimbostratus clouds. The weather was so perfect for sleep and the blankets were inviting. The temptation to sleep and postpone the trip was creeping, but I had to subdue it. I quickly took a passport-sized bath as we called it, wiping my face and my armpits with a damp towel. I hung my untidily packed backpack on my right hand shoulder and hit the road on foot. The cold breeze and rain showers swept away every remnant of heat in the atmosphere. Nothing could stop my determination, not even the rain.

Neither had I an umbrella nor a raincoat, but my dark blue bomber jacket was versatile, with a silky material on its outer layer that deferred raindrops from sinking through. On the inside, it had a thick and warm fleece-like material, which warmed my upper body from feeling the cold breeze that froze my legs. The showers subsided as I walked further away from the village.

The ungraded roads were wet and slippery such that I preferred walking on the wet grassy areas beside the roads. As I approached Hingwe village, showers of rain began to diminish and the weather became warmer with smooth and milky fog suspending in the air and on the earth's surface. I could not see objects beyond a 50-metre radius.

I had left the village very early in the morning to cross over to Botswana before the border patrol officers started sniffing around the border fence to arrest illegal immigrants. Botswana is generally a strict country with strict laws, it's not easy to bribe an officer in Botswana as it is in Zimbabwe and South Africa. The Tswana are law-abiding citizens and do not compromise on that. The country is one of the worst in Southern Africa when it comes to handling crime suspects. On the extreme end, it is considered as one of the safest countries in Africa because of its crimelessness. I suppose how you see the country is dependent on the side of the law you are in.

I crossed Maitengwe River before the sun's rays could torch the ground, circumventing areas I suspected were bound to be patrolled on. I boarded my first taxi in Mbalambi, headed for Francistown. It was very easy for me to blend in like a chameleon in Botswana as most residents spoke Kalanga, my mother tongue. It is said that the Kalanga of Zimbabwe and those of Botswana were once a large ethnic group that was separated by the erection of colonial territorial borders between the two countries. Their separation earned them a minority status in both countries. This probably explains why we have relatives on the other side of the border. The Kalanga's residence across two countries gave rise to a history of trans-border relations and disintegrated family ties.

I dropped off in Francistown and decided to stay for two weeks while doing piece jobs to fundraise for my trip to South Africa. During my stay in Francistown I met three gentlemen I trained with in Zambia, they were also enroute to South Africa. We decided to travel together and set a date.

Apparently, a gold mine in South Africa called Venterspost in the western side of Johannesburg was hiring foreigners and once employed, the employers created legal documents for their employees to work in the country. Venterspost it was. We were going to try our luck at the mine until we find our feet in South Africa. None of us knew where the hell Venterspost was. There is an African proverb translating to 'he who has a mouth will never get lost', so we prepared to manoeuvre our way to the gold mine, come rain come thunder.

It was exactly after two weeks of my arrival in Francistown that we boarded a taxi to Lobatse, a town near the Botswana Pioneer border post. From Lobatse we walked through the bushes at midnight, crossing the border fence incognito. After crossing the border, we walked for about a mile until we reached the main road from the Pioneer border post to Zeerust town in South Africa. We hitchhiked to Zeerust, then Mafikeng where we stopped for refreshments and rested for few hours until dawn.

The easiest mode of transport for us was the train. We avoided roads, as there were a lot of roadblocks and we could be arrested for being in the country illegally. South Africa was still under the Apartheid administration and the movement of Black people between towns was closely monitored. At exactly 5:30am in the morning, we had already bought tickets at the packed Mafikeng train station. Within few minutes, I could hear the train coming from a distance and my stomach was queasy as I anticipated my first ever ride to Johannesburg. I had heard so much about the city of Johannesburg; it was apparently a melting pot of milk, bile and honey. I was dressed in my finest regalia, which was basically a clean pair of hand-me-down pants and a shirt that was minus holes and stains.

As the Shosholoza Meyl train approached, I felt its vibrations as it came closer and closer. I really had no idea of the prospects that lay ahead. As it came to a complete halt, I only had a minute to manoeuvre my tiny self into the train and find a spot before the train left the station. Other compartments were filled beyond capacity and people were hanging off the outside, clinging for their dear lives. It was insane to think that I could find a space to grab hold, but I had to or stay behind behind. Luckily, no one was left behind. We were headed to Johannesburg, *die plek van goud* (the city of gold), commonly known as Egoli. We were not sure where exactly the gold mine was located, but for every black Zimbabwean from the western side of the country, we referred to the whole of the present day Gauteng as Egoli, we did not know the demarcations.

I vividly remembered the stories Nkust would tell us as children about Egoli, how much he managed to outwit the Johannesburg criminals, manoeuvre the *tsotsi*-infested city unharmed and made money from hustling on the streets. I was going to be like Nkust, all my dreams would finally come true.

Having been to Botswana, Zambia, Angola and of course Zimbabwe, I must say South Africa had the most advanced infrastructure at the time. Roads were beautifully built, trains travelled on time, and cities were beyond beautiful.

A juxtaposition of fear and excitement pre-occupied me along the journey. I was excited to be on the move, yet I had no concept of what the future held. It was the beginning of an adventure. I felt no hunger and the passing of time was external, not felt in that moment. I did not feel it when the train stopped. I did not really notice the many towns we passed, I lived only in my mind. I wouldn't have cared about the journey, all I cared about were the prospects that lay ahead. '*Egoli!*' the train conductor shouted, '*sesifikile*' before I knew it, we had arrived. The fantasy had stopped, it was now real. I felt myself trembling from the inside but I had to be strong. I pulled myself together, wore a bold face, took my bag and stepped off the train.

We disembarked the train at the train station adjacent to Johannesburg Park Station. I recalled our enquiry for directions at Mafikeng train station; we were supposed to catch another train from Johannesburg station to Randfontein. I had written the name on a piece of paper, as I did not trust my memory with English words. The train conductor assisted with directions of where we were to board the connecting train. Within a few minutes, we were headed to Randfontein. The train took about an hour to arrive at the destination, and we took a taxi to the mine.

Upon arrival, we stutteringly informed the security guard at the mine entrance that we were looking for jobs. He did not respond verbally, but through hand signals, directing us to a building entirely made of corrugated zinc. The building seemed to have many compartments inside, serving as office spaces I assumed.

"We are looking for a job sir", Cobra, the bravest amongst us uttered those words to a broad-shouldered and middleweight Umlungu standing in front of the building. He forgot to at least extend some greetings, I supposed. English has the capacity to rob one of their friendliness as they can only verbalize what they crammed, which is usually the main message. Greetings are secondary and besides Abelungu don't usually take offence when one omits the greeting episode, in fact they prefer one to hit the snake on the head and get straight to the point.

Umlungu laughed sarcastically looking at me. "Even this little boy wants a job?" he asked. My demeanor had always been problematic; it would make me miss opportunities. Little did Umlungu know that I was a former freedom fighter and had killed Abelungu during the war of liberation. While we were still thinking of the right English words to explain to Umlungu that I was not a little boy, he instructed us to take off our clothes.

What? Why? We could not understand; we were looking for jobs not stripping for Umlungu. We failed to hide our discomfiture and we gazed at each other wide-eyed. "You are looking for jobs, so you have to undergo the checking process boys", Umlungu said.

We were listening carefully this time around, trying to stomach and decode what Umlungu meant, as it sounded ludicrous. Perhaps our ears had initially played tricks on us. The mischievous smile on his face indicated that he was enjoying and rejoicing at this unscrupulous act of robbing us of our manhood by asking us to undress outside the building as he stood by the entrance.

We simultaneously felt a tad of uneasy but we had no choice but to comply with the checking process and undress as wild as the undressing act was. We entered the first room naked and went through the checking process one by one. Each room had an X-ray-like machine, so we were scanned at three different rooms and Umlungu was recording the results. God knows what was being checked because even to date I am still clueless. After this ghastly procedure, we were employed.

There was however neither immediate disclosure of the contracts nor the salaries. It sounded like a verbal pact kind of employment where the employee had no power to engage the employment terms and package. We had no choice but to be grateful for such luck in a foreign land. Our names were written down and our fingerprints taken to facilitate the application of legal documents/passbooks that proved that we were mineworkers and legal in the country.

After we completed the process, we were taken to *ehostela* (hostel) where we would reside for the duration of our employment at the mine. Ehostela was a male only residential block reserved for men working in the mines at the time. These men came predominantly from different provinces such as the former Transkei and Ciskei (present day Eastern Cape), KwaZulu Natal, Mpumalanga and countries such as Malawi, Zambia and Mozambique.

We were shown a small room that we were to share with five other men. The hostel was horrifyingly appalling to live in, it was extremely filthy and it smelt foul. How could eight grown men share a single room without a bed even? There were two kitchens infested with green bomber flies and shared by a huge number of hostel dwellers. The bathrooms were an open space where 50 men would bath at the same time using buckets. The thought of sharing an open plan bathroom with other men was somewhat dehumanizing. A grown man needed privacy.

Dwelling in the hostel with people of different cultural backgrounds was energy zapping. One had to learn how to understand and tolerate each of the different ethnic groups represented there. The Zulus for instance, were territorial and very violent. It was easy for them to pull a knife upon a small argument; hence, our sensors were always up during our conversations with them. Xhosa people were very talkative, one could not win an argument with them but they weren't as violent. The other groups such as the Sotho, Tswana and Pedi were peaceful and we never really crossed paths. Foreigners on the other hand knew their place; they were mostly timid, kept to themselves and avoided any form of confrontation with locals.

After a week of staying ehostela, I thought of the biblical verse from Genesis 2:18, which says, "The Lord God said, it is not good for the man to be alone. I would make a helper suitable for him". Although I was not really sure of my Christianity, my stay ehostela made me realize that indeed it is not good for men to be alone, men need women. They need helpers to give them a sense of direction, assist them in making the right life choices and calm their often-animalistic behaviors. Fights were rampant ehostela; dwellers would occasionally stab each other over silly arguments such as cleaning and general misunderstandings. Dwellers mostly mismanaged their money by buying alcohol and paying prostitutes until they ran out of money to buy food. This resulted in theft and more fights.

Most men staying ehostela were married back home, but could not bring their wives and children to live with them. Other than it being prohibited, there was no space to accommodate families. The only chance most mineworkers got to visit their families was in December. As a result, infidelity was almost inevitable and most mineworkers had sex with prostitutes who often serviced a lot of ehostela dwellers rotationally. I am proud of myself for not falling into that trap. Although I had needs as a man, I felt that the sexual intersection was pathetic and contracting diseases was inevitable.

We reported to the mine the following day and received our contracts (one-year contract each) and the salary inscribed on the contract was R20 a month. We were not accustomed to the value of the South African Rand but from the money we had spent on the road, we knew that amount was too small to be a monthly salary. We were however grateful to have gotten jobs without much of a hustle. On the first two days on the job, we were taught about first aid. It was crucial as we were going to nurse each other in times of emergency. Although I was not given any formal qualification or document indicating that I completed a first aid course, I am confident to include that experience on my CV. After the first aid training, we were taught rock drilling. Rock drilling was going to be our job description for as long as we were employed at the gold mine.

I almost quit my job upon realizing how deep and dangerous the mineshaft was. Abelungu used lifts to go down the mine and back to the surface. Every Black person used their feet and ropes to go down the mineshaft and come back to the surface. When we started our jobs, we were each given three injections on the chest for bravery to go down the mineshaft. I'm not sure what drug was used to instill that sense of bravery but it worked. No one in their sober senses would go down that mineshaft daily without a sedative in their system. We eventually got accustomed to the job and it became less scary.

The working conditions were very appalling at the mine and injuries were inevitable. To date, I have scars all over my body as a result of mine injuries. Mine workers who got injured/crippled on the job were dismissed to go back to their villages of origin without any package. A number of mine workers died underground due to injuries or respiratory problems caused by chemicals or particles from mining and drilling rocks. Those who died were immediately replaced and co-workers were not given a chance to mourn their colleagues or at least travel for burials. I imagined that if I had died, I would have been buried like a dog as my family did not know my whereabouts and I had no relative close by.

We persevered nonetheless as we had nowhere else to go. When the year ended, our contracts were renewed but salaries were never increased. On one fateful day while we were drilling rocks in the mineshaft, a sharp stone teared off from the larger rock, flew towards my right leg, and sharply cut my hamstring muscle. The incident happened within a split second, I could not dodge the stone. I had never felt so much pain in my life. My leg felt numb and I thought I would never walk again. For the first time that day, I was taken up to the surface using Abelungu's lift. I was eventually admitted at the hospital and had my wound cleaned, treated and sewn. I was discharged after four days but could still not walk properly. I was limping and almost dragging my right foot.

After I got discharged from the hospital, I had to report for duty in that condition, otherwise I would face dismissal. The more I went down the shaft, the more the wound opened up again. It had not healed. I failed to work with a fresh and excruciating wound. I was taken to the surface using a lift for the second time.

I would never forget that day as I was thrashed by Umlungu who accused me of tearing off my wound on purpose as a way of dodging work. My blood boiled and I gnashed my teeth to suppress my anger, otherwise I would have retaliated and things would have gotten ugly. I had never experienced such callousness in my whole life. How could I tear off my would when I was in so much pain?

I was taken to hospital and had the wound sewn again until it finally healed. We worked at Venterspost mine with our contracts yearly renewed until the dawn of freedom in South Africa. On one eventful day, as Black mine workers, we decided to protest for salary increment. We could not afford to provide remittances to our families. We could only buy food with our salaries, pay rentals ehostela and nothing else. We were practically surviving from hand to mouth.

At the time, Black protests in the country were rife as a fierce resistance against the brutality and segregation of the Apartheid government. The protests had sparked international attention. We were certain that the protest was a quixotic one, but we took a leap of faith nonetheless, hoping that our employer would hear our plea, avoid any form of negative publicity of the mine and come to a negotiation table with us.

In less than an hour into the protest, all of us who were protesting were arrested and sent to jail for engaging in what Abelungu called a "violent protest". The arrest was very hard to stomach. As far as I remember, the protest was a peaceful march but the legal proceedings favored Abelungu. The law was commiserating with Abelungu and it was part of the vicious state apparatus. We were sent to jail where we spent about 21 days.

After our release, we were fired and blacklisted from working at any mine in South Africa. Our passbooks were stamped red, signaling that we could not work anywhere else. At that moment, things seemed to be happening in a cinematic slow motion; it resembled a déjà vu and appeared like something not supposed to be happening at that particular moment. My heart was pounding, I was shaking, my palms were sweating and my knees were knocking against each other. How were we going to survive? We were back to square one. We needed jobs, we needed to eat, we needed to have a decent lifestyle.

We had to think on our feet of the next move with my fellow countrymen whom we met in Francistown enroute to South Africa. Cobra had a plan, he was the cleverest, we had to swallow our pride and admit it for progress sake. He suggested that we board a train to Johannesburg. Cobra's uncle who was once residing at a servant's quota (a small room) at a flat's rooftop in a Johannesburg city called Hillbrow was now jointly renting the flat to buy. Apparently, Umlungu who owned that flat had relocated to England when news of the release of Nelson Mandela spread. His release was a threat to Abelungu who were uncertain of their future should a Black man be in power. Therefore, Cobra's uncle took advantage of his employer's reasonably cheap property and collaboratively bought it with few other Black men to rent out rooms. Times were indeed changing in South Africa; Black people were beginning to own property.

We boarded the train to Johannesburg the following day to try to hunt for jobs and eke out a living. We disembarked at the train station near Johannesburg Park Station. As soon as we stepped out of the train, I began hearing different tongues, which I was certain were not South African languages. People spoke different languages and seemed as busy as bees. The city centre was full of activity with people pushing trolleys with loads of luggage from trains, others selling different goods, stretching from vegetables, fruits, second hand clothes, cigarettes, sweets and anything tradable. It was difficult to maneuver the packed city centre. Surprisingly, there were no Abelungu in the city centre as I had anticipated. What had happened to the Johannesburg city centre I had heard of and imagined, which was strictly for Abelungu? I asked myself in a silent soliloquy.

Cobra had been to Johannesburg before and he knew quite a number of countrymen who stayed in Hillbrow, other than his uncle, so he led the way. At the time, a sense of fraternity and brotherhood existed, people sheltered each other before others could get their feet into the game.

We walked to Hillbrow via Smit street, turned on Klein street, then Pretoria street, then Edith Cavell street, Twist street, Quartz and then Claim street. We were headed to one of the tallest flats in Hillbrow. We walked silently in a straight line, one after the other. We were awkwardly tailing Cobra who knew Hillbrow like the back of his hand. He led the way. Although we were a squad of four men, one could not help but notice that the atmosphere was hair-raising and the air was thick with tension. The street inhabitants seemed very comfortable in such a frightening environment. Screams of crying and defiant children punctured the activity of the city. Unsupervised children were roaming aimlessly down the streets and teenage girls strapped babies on their backs, having had them while they were babies themselves. Most faces seemed hungry with neither energy nor vigor except for their roaming and alert eyes.

The eyes of people who stood by the street corners were too piercing not to notice, and suspicious. Each of those people seemed to be having some kind of a weapon visible and protruding on the belt of their pants. Even pigeons carried switchblades.

Most of these people drank some form of liquid from khaki bags. They appeared to belong to territorial gang groups although they stood haphazardly, seriously surveying and scrutinizing new faces and targeting faces worth robbing. My body would jump, responding to every sound and movement in the vicinity. Even a mere cough could just as often be a series of signal of violence. Knowing which cough was survival happened unconsciously when one's cells had been acclimated to the environment. My sense of danger was overwhelming.

Hillbrow is a rundown, densely populated, *tsotsi*-infested and highly notorious place in the heart of Johannesburg where you find most of the province's street ragamuffins with a rugged way of life. It harbours foreign nationals and many shady characters because of its cheaper accommodation and convenience to people working in the Johannesburg CBD. It is a place where young people do the unthinkable to earn a living. Its lawlessness makes it a hotbed of gangsters and drug addicts' paradise. Alcohol and drugs are sold on every corner. The place is dangerous by day as it is at nightfall.

Some of its tenements looked as if they would drop to the ground from exhaustion while some seemed empty and dark with no sign of inhabitants. There was trash all over the streets and some buildings were rundown with the occasional drunk or possibly addicted people stumbling out of one of them.

A young ragged man, tattooed with an eagle on the side of his neck approached us from the side. He was spring walking as if he had sore burns underneath his feet. I only realised that his step was actually in tune with the latest rap number that was blasting out of an upstairs window. His sweat and body odours assaulted our nostrils as he came closer. His hands were behind his back in a palm-in-palm gesture, displaying a sense of fearlessness and confidence in what he was about to do. Something was definitely about to go down, I felt it from the pit of my belly.

I resisted the urge to flee and concealed my discomfort. Timidity in my mind immobilized me. My body stiffened. I felt like I was trapped in a spell and could not move. *"Sanibona majita, nisiphatheleni la?"* he asked. My shirt clung to my back, absorbing what sweat it could. Then a dusty light breeze blew, bringing the smell of slate urine and evaporating the moisture on my shirt. Before we could respond, a cat-like rat ran past, between his legs, scurrying into the nearby drain filled with litter and beer bottles. That is when he displayed his vulnerability, although he tried to suppress it. He had not seen the rat coming, and its hugeness was beyond ordinary, even *inja yegame* (dog of the game) could not help but scream for dear life. We are all human beings after all; we all have adrenaline rush that we often fail to suppress in frightening situations. I guess the giant rat had saved our terrified asses. We kept on walking and the young man took several seconds to recover from the rat saga. By the time he got himself together, we were out of sight.

We finally arrived at the building, after 15 minutes of walking. I finally got a sense of security as soon as we climbed the stairs of the flat. So much had happened within that short space of time. Cobra's uncle and his wife welcomed us warmly in their bedroom apartment partitioned into two by a curtain. The wife prepared a meal for us while we took turns to shower. After the meal and shower, we all fell into a deep slumber and woke up around 6pm. By the time we woke up, people who spoke different languages, stretching from isiZulu, Yoruba, isiXhosa, Sepedi, Venda and Nyanja, filled the apartment to the brim. I was familiar with Nyanja from my stay in Zambia. Although I had never heard of Yoruba before, I knew the language was foreign. But how could so many people live in such a small apartment?

In my head, I began questioning Cobra's uncle' ownership of that flat yet he lived under such conditions. When I initially head of ownership, I had romanticised it and had a colour television picture of it. I later learnt that no Black domestic workers could afford to buy such a flat and live normally, they had to overpopulate it with tenants to be able to afford the monthly instalments to the seller.

They had however taken a leap of faith to make that decision, as they would eventually own it after paying off the entire amount. The seller also made a bait with his property, trusting Black men who could not afford a bank bond to finance them. Times had changed indeed, there wasn't any Umlungu willing to buy property in Hillbrow anymore, it was now a Black man's territory, hence, sellers had no option but to sell to Black people.

All bedrooms in the apartment were partitioned and shared by different families. The bedroom that Cobra's uncle and his wife used was shared with the Zambian family. They used the other side of the curtain. When sleep time came, Cobra's uncle and his wife slept on the three-quarter sized bed and the four of us slept on the floor. The side of the bedroom was so small that the bed was placed on top of four metal five-litre cans of paint filled with cement mortar. These five litre containers were used to uplift the bed and elongate the space underneath to act as both storage and space for visitors to sleep on.

The night was torturous, as we had to listen to the Zambian man and his wife making love behind the curtain. It sounded as though they were doing their best to be considerate of roommates and supress their moaning, but the woman failed to hold it in, and her lovemaking noises intensified. What annoyed me the most was the sound produced by the noisy squeaky bed.

We had to vacate that place as soon as possible I thought to myself. It was unlivable. Our stay would compromise Cobra's uncle and his wife's lovemaking. I can only wonder how they overcame the temptation to make love that night with the seductive love sounds coming from beyond the curtain.

We stayed for 2 days in Hillbrow and we then decided to join Cobra's old friends who worked as garden boys at Northcliff. Northcliff was an affluent residential suburb whose residents were largely Abelungu. Black people residing there were usually helpers living in the servants' quotas. We were going to squat in one of Umlungu's servant quotas.

The atmosphere at Northcliff was different, quiet and peaceful compared to Hillbrow. The houses were large and standalone with perfect landscaping. The houses were all gated extravagant high-walled mansions with electric wires walls to keep non-residents and trespassers out of sight. Armed security personnel patrolled the streets and confronted any suspicious looking people or those roaming the streets aimlessly.

Tagwisa waited for us outside the house. I suppose he didn't want our arrival to disturb his bosses or cause any form of chaos with the security guards. Before we could enter the yard, he briefed us with the rules of the house and of the neighbourhood. Tagwisa stayed with his brother in an old garage turned to be a servant's quota. Fortunately, the garage was a standalone residence and had no connection with the main house. The owner of the house had renovated his house and built another garage adjacent to the house. Tagwisa and his brother used another gate different from his bosses'. The plan was that we were to stay there secretly without Umlungu noticing our presence.

The bathroom and the servants' toilet were outside, so we would only bath and relieve ourselves when the coast was clear. We could not jeopardise Tagwisa's job and risk being homeless. We even had to supress our cough, and sneeze with timing lest the homeowner suspected that there were more people living in his yard.

We stayed at Northcliff for two weeks. One day, Petros, Tagwisa's brother had gone out of the yard marketing for a job with three of his friends who stayed in the neighbourhood. Immigration officers who asked to see their identity documents stopped them. Three of Petros' friends outran the Immigration Officers, while Petros was caught. Instead of going to jail alone, Petros told the officers that there were other undocumented immigrants in the house and showed them where we were.

We were arrested immediately. Tagwisa luckily dodged the arrest as he was in the toilet at the time. We were taken to Leeuwkop prison. Before the end of the week, the crew that I was imprisoned with were bailed by their relatives and were set free. I was the only one with no one to call my own in Johannesburg. I stayed for two months at Leeuwkop prison. After two months, I was deported to Beitbridge in Zimbabwe, and then taken to Ross Camp in Mzilikazi, Bulawayo. From Ross Camp, we were taken to Khami where I served 5 months in prison.

None of my family members back home knew what had befallen me. There was no means of communication at the time. I supposed my girlfriend Benkoe had moved on with her life. Upon my release, I decided to go home, consult my ancestors and have medicine men perform some cleansing to cast out all the spells of bad luck engulfing my life.

I stayed home for about a week. Home was unlivable. I had to look for a job somewhere and fend for Gogo; she was getting frail by the day. I also had a child that I had to take care of. I left home again heading for Johannesburg via Francistown, Botswana. As soon as I disembarked the taxi at Johannesburg park station, three immigration officers stopped me and asked for my identification document. I had none. I tried negotiating but in vain.

Of the three officers, one was Black and two were Abelungu. The Black officer seemed to sympathise with me. "*Akungikhulumele mfowethu*", I begged him to advocate for me to Abelungu. Unfortunately, his hands were tied and law was law. His response gave my heart a sudden jolt and un-wanted tears pricked my eyes. I was handcuffed and put in a police van. My life was as stagnant as a pool of water. Would I ever walk free? In Zimbabwe, I was a fugitive, In South Africa I was an illegal immigrant.

I was taken back to Leeuwkop prison. I spent one night in remand. On the second day, I was to appear in court. I was taken out of the cell by three police officers to go to court. Upon disembarking the police van at the doorstep of the court, an opportunity presented itself when the police officer who had just removed my handcuffs bent on his knee to tie his shoelace. I capitalised on the opportunity and took to my heels. I knew I was a sprinter, but my body was trembling with fear. What if I got shot in the process?

I was frantically running for my life but somehow my legs felt like concrete. I tried to run as fast as I could but I felt like my feet were paralysed and numb. It must have been the exhaustion from travelling. Other than the fatigue getting the best of me, it was the fear of being on the wrong side of the law that was dragging my body to move in a somewhat slow motion. The police officers chased me as soon as I exited the court gate. The first officer was quickly eating the area between us. The distance between us was getting smaller and smaller with each breath I took. My body was failing me.

I took a left turn on the first left street and ran as fast as I could, although my fast was not good enough. My arms were swinging exchangeable to the back and front, creating a tempo for my legs to carry me through. I felt my heart pounding extremely fast and my ear momentarily clogged my brain as I launched onto the street at my full speed.

I knew I was doomed upon realising that the street I turned onto had a dead end, it had no exit. I was a few seconds from colliding with a brick wall. The cops zeroed in towards me, I had no option, but to halt my run. I bent my body and let my hands rest on my knees and took two deep breaths, in through my nose and out through my mouth. The cool mid-morning breeze coursed through my lungs and dried my already patched throat. After wiping away sweat on my forehead with my bare hands, I lifted both my hands to surrender. I was petrified to the point of passing out. I had committed the gravest mistake of my life, jeopardising my chances of freedom.

As soon as I was handcuffed, the police started kicking, slapping and raining rapid-fire punches on me. I felt a sudden flood of adrenaline, as the beatings were a surprise act. I had not imagined that an unarmed and handcuffed criminal could be a victim of police brutality. How could a group of muscular police officers kick a man when he was down? I was helpless and could not protect myself with my hands handcuffed. I could only exaggerate my pain by groaning and screaming. The severest punch on my tummy left me at the verge of throwing up. I dropped my head and body forward to protect my stomach from further punches.

One officer kicked me from behind and I landed hard on the ground. I mistakenly bit my tongue in the process and swallowed the metallic taste of my blood. While I lay helpless on the ground, the officer suddenly lunged at me, punching and kicking me on my ribs. I skilfully rolled myself on the ground as I was trained back in Zambia, dodging and repelling some of his fists and kicks. One police officer said, '*Staan op jou bleddie buitelander*' translating to 'stand up you bloody foreigner'.

I struggled to stand on my feet until one officer came to my aid. We eventually arrived at the court gate where I was shoved into the police van like a dog. The court case was cancelled with immediate effect and I was taken to Sun City prison. Of all the prisons I had been at, Sun City was the most ruthless, with prisoners who would randomly beat, stab and even kill fellow prisoners like they were slaughtering chicken. The cruelty was unbearable. I stayed at Sun City prison for three weeks. From Sun City, I was transferred to John Foster police station where I was to be deported again to Zimbabwe.

On the day I was to be deported, I lied to the police officers that I had bags I had to fetch in Hillbrow before being deported. The officers drove me to Hillbrow, while on the road, I saw two men I knew from home who bribed the police officers with R20 and they set me free. I narrowly escaped the second deportation. I spent two weeks in Hillbrow but I was never comfortable there. I witnessed a gruesome robbery gone wrong through the window of the flat I shared with the lads who had rescued me by bribing the police. From that day on, I decided that I had to leave that place.

In robbery situations in Hillbrow, victims became helpless with no choice but to surrender all their possessions in order to save their lives. Screaming would not help, as the robbery episode would not clarify who is the predator and who is the prey in the process. Even robbers and thieves would in some instances scream during a robbery and play victim. Onlookers would just watch and proceed with their journeys as if nothing out of the ordinary happened. Poverty evoked beast like characters from human beings and took away their remorse and sanity.

In some instances, community members and passer-bys would get tired of such inhumane and evil behaviours, take matters into their own hands, and uproot these fiends from the human race altogether. Although ghettos are a difficult place to live in, sometimes the underlying unity, comradery and a deep sense of unity exists. Mob justice cases often resulted in the unaccountable death of perpetrators. By the time the sounds of police sirens would be heard, everyone would disappear from the scene. Police would be greeted by the corpse lying in a pool of blood.

Almost every corner of the buildings in Hillbrow had five things, a hooker, a liquor store, a gun-shop, graffiti on concrete walls and a small cafeteria selling Nigerian dishes whose foul smell engulfed the entire street. Their stew would be a mixture of several hot spices, dried vegetables and dried fish. Although the smell of these dishes was uninviting, the irony was that the food actually tasted like heaven. In most cases, the Nigerian cafeterias would be just a disguise of the core drug-dealing business operating behind the scenes. People living in such areas did not easily sell each other out, everyone knew everyone and everyone knew where to buy drugs. Even an ice cream man could be covertly selling drugs. Only the street smart could survive in Hillbrow.

CHAPTER 9

The past demands an emotional ransom

After my bribery bail-out, I decided to go back to Northcliff. In suburbs, there was a better chance of landing a gardening job than in Hillbrow. In Hillbrow, it was survival of the fittest and I could not blend into such an environment as sober as I was. Other than the unfortunate incident of being arrested by the immigration officers in Northcliff and having to hide from Umlungu, the environment was peaceful. I squatted in Tagwisa's room while marketing for my own job.

I finally got a weekend gardening job 7 houses from Tagwisa's place. The job was not fulltime, so there was no stay-in accommodation. I continued staying with Tagwisa undercover. We stroke a deal, he provided accommodation and I bought all the groceries needed. In most instances, Tagwisa ate at the main house, although he occasionally complained that his bosses enjoyed tasteless and light vegetables. He was a Black man; he wanted solid food like pap and umngqusho to fill and sit in his tummy for quite some time, not the leaves he was served with. He often complained that they cooked semi-raw eggs and undone steak that was disgusting to eat.

After about a month of my stay in Northcliff, I started having weird dreams at night and visions of peculiar images by day. It was like the incidences that had happened in the past were coming back to life as real as they had happened. They felt so real that I felt my head spinning whenever I tried to understand what was going on.

I started seeing Pit Bull crazily barking at me. I would shake my head to try to awaken my senses. In my subconscious mind, I was kind of aware that this had happened before and shouldn't be happening now. The more I tried to dodge Pit Bull; his voice would drum in my ears more pronounced.

I began hearing sounds of guns being fired, voice overs from the ova-ovas, commanding us to shoot, retaliate or abort the mission. I was losing control of my body and my thoughts. The most haunting nightly dream I had was of the Hurungwe ambush where I shot and killed a man. He was not the first person I had ever shot, but there was something disturbing and haunting about how he died.

We were running low on ammunition, so we were careful to be precise at the enemy and shoot only on the dangerous parts of the body. I knelt down on the lower ground of where I was hiding behind the thick bushes. I positioned my AK-47 upright, pointing at the enemy. I let the gun rest on its grip. My left hand held the machine's magazine, while my right pulled the trigger. I closed one eye to let the other follow the bullet fire without destruction. The bullet went straight to its target's chest as intended.

As soon as it hit him, he staggered for a second, then held his left chest where the bullet had pierced through. He gawked at the direction where the bullet had come from. I was in hiding but he seemed to look straight into my pupil. His eyes were piercing as if they were communicating something. He then took his eyes off me and looked at his bleeding wound on the chest and tried to bandage it with his shirt. Within a split second, he spit a mouthful of blood and momentarily staggered as if he became dizzy. He then fell to the ground in a slow motion and died.

I wasn't a stone cold killer, we were at war, and at war people die, but I would never forget the look the dying man gave me before departing. It was so disturbing that I felt guilty from the pit of my belly. Why would a human being be on a mission to kill another human being?

Before I lost my marbles, I don't remember recalling precise war events, but my insane self seemed to have a photographic memory. Every time I would wake up from my dreams of horrifying events, I would try to re-summon myself together but in vain. I was haunted by my past, at the same time, I was trying too hard to dodge this insanity, it was worse than death. I subconsciously knew that something was amiss with my behaviour and my thoughts. Tagwisa was as equally confused as I was, but he tried to calm me down. I suppose he feared that if my insanity escalated to the point of my stay with him being noticed by his employer, he would be fired for bringing a stranger into the yard.

I began experiencing memory lapses, started becoming somnambulant and my bad dreams continued. During the day, I would see things that my subconscious mind thought were unreal. Surprisingly, I would sometimes get back to my normal senses and that is when I realised that I needed help, I needed a form of divination from above, or I needed to appease those below. But how was I to do that in a foreign land?

Tagwisa organised with fellow countrymen close by and they decided to take me to a Zion church, one of them worshipped at. Zimbabweans predominantly led the church, hence attracting other countrymen. Many people had received divine healing in church and most of their problems were solved as they confessed in church or were prayed for. Tagwisa hired a van to transport us to a Zion branch in Soweto on a Sunday morning. The van was an ideal transport for a mentally disturbed person. When I would start hallucinating, they would tie my hands to my back and hold me together.

We disembarked the van a few yards from the church. I was as sober as a judge when we arrived. I could hear the congregants singing familiar songs aloud. Upon arriving at the church doorstep, we removed our shoes. This is custom at Zion churches. It's observed as a sign of reverence. The concept of removing shoes was borrowed from the Biblical Moses in the Old Testament who removed his sandals when he was about to enter a Holy place in Mount Sinai. As we got into the church building, which was a rented classroom at a pre-school, a praise session was underway.

> *Sizomchapha kanjani umfula u Jordan*
> *singavumanga zonke izono zethu.*
> *Thulu lulululu lulu lululu*
> *lulu*
> *lululu lululu lulu.*

The song loosely translates to, "How are we going to cross the Jordan River without confessing our sins?"

Most of the songs sung were neither praise nor worship as the contemporary Pentecostal songs sung today. Zionic songs in those days were just about any incident in the bible. Whether it was good or negative, as long it was in the bible, it could be converted to a hymn and sung in church. Congregants wore gown-like robes of different colours, green, blue and white with small stripes of different colours on the sleeves, belt and the lower bottom. This dress code resembled that of Aaron as instructed by God in the book of Exodus 28.

Both men and women wore the same robes; the only difference was that men wore white trousers underneath their robes, while women and girls wore doeks to cover their heads. The head covering is a Biblical teaching that was given by Paul in his first letter to the Corinthians (1 Corinthians 11).

During praise and worship, young men and women engaged in their ritual circle dance, rhythmic to the drumbeats. A team of three young men and a young woman engaged in the drum-beating onus. Each of these drums had a different sound (soprano, turner, alto and bass) that blended perfectly to form a musical rhythm, food to one's ear.

Although the entire church seemed to be singing, a group of young people standing on one corner seemed to be part of a church choir that led the singing. Another group of young people enclosed the centre of the building performing their circle dance. In this dance, each dancer would spin round and round and swirling their robes rhythmically, creating a surreal scene. Apparently, the spinning signifies getting lost into the spiritual realm just like Elijah who was taken to heaven by a whirlwind in the book of 2 Kings 2.

Their spinning would get faster and faster as the singing and the drumming intensified. This spinning would cause one to feel dizzy, hence "venturing into the Holy of hollies". In Zion churches, the spirit is not merely a concept but is very real and experiential. One had to feel it in that dizzy moment.

Male figures carried rods, which upon enquiry, I was told that they were used to combat any form of evil and perform miracles upon hopeless situations. The rod concept was inspired by the Biblical Moses whose rod was used mightily to prove his power to Pharaoh and also perform miracles. Moses' rod turned into snake at some point. When Moses and his people were thirsty at the desert of Zin, he struck a rock twice with his rod and water gushed out for people and livestock to drink (Numbers 20). When the Israelites were being pursued by the Egyptians and reached a dead end at the Red Sea, Moses held his rod high and the red sea parted into half. The Israelites safely went through. The rod performed miracles as Moses yielded to the voice of God. Thus, the Zionists' rods were believed to perform miracles the same way they did with Moses.

As the young men' spinning intensified, they would eventually fall to the floor and they would be put in the centre of the building. All those who fell were believed to be demon possessed and would do snake-like devilish moves and begin to speak in funny tongues. Pastors, deacons and other highly esteemed church leaders began to cast out demons by praying for the possessed and started beating them with Moses' rod until the demons departed. I vividly remember one deacon who prayed loudly with his face just inches away from the face of the demon-possessed woman laying on the floor. The deacon' saliva drizzled on the woman's face disgustingly in that demon-casting episode.

I understood little about spiritual issues, but it seemed fashionable for congregants to manifest demons. I never understood what demons were. I knew that evil spirits existed but couldn't differentiate them with the demons that were cast out in church.

The sermon was on 'The forerunner: John the Baptist'. The Preacher spoke at length about the birth of John the Baptist and his mission of preaching about the coming of Jesus Christ. As the Preacher finished his sermon, it was time for testimonies. So, since things were done according to the book, whoever was giving a testimony had to quote at least a sentence from the Preacher's preaching to prove that he/she was attentive. Anything one could take home from the sermon. Since the preaching was on the birth of John the Baptist, Deacon Mhlanga stood up to testify. As a norm, he had no choice but to begin by quoting the Preacher's word. He cleared his throat and said, *"Amen Bazalwane. Bazalwane lizwile ukuthi u Johane wayeloboya..."* This loosely translates to, "Amen Brethren. Brethren, I hope you heard the Preacher saying John the Baptist was hairy...” This provided some comic relief to the otherwise dull service. How could the whole 'deacon' quote such a statement from the entire 1hr 30 minutes of preaching? I guess he was one of those lukewarm and spiritually crippled church leaders.

Brethren are naturally quick to judge, aren't they? Mind you, I also could not remember much from the preaching except that the birth of John the Baptist was a fulfilment of prophecy. This particular statement was what the Preacher hammered into our brains after every interval of preaching, pitching his voice loudly like a football commentator when the ball is in the 18 area.

After testimonies, there was a call for those who wanted to be prayed for. I hesitated. I wasn't sure if I should go up-front or not. I felt healed in the entire two hours we spent in church. I had not hallucinated or seen weird visions ever since I arrived. Knowing my plight, Tagwisa held my hand and led me straight to the centre of the church, which I as-sume was the prayer altar. I was forever grateful for Tagwisa for standing by my side when I lost touch with reality and occasionally lost my sanity. In such situations, people tend to judge one without knowing the circumstances surrounding their unorthodox behaviour. Tagwisa never judged me or made fun of me, never mind that we were not related. I met him through a friend but he became closer than a brother.

At the altar, Tagwisa whispered to the church Pastor what my problem was. Just when I thought my spokesperson had explained everything, the Pastor turned to me to ask exactly what I was seeing in my dreams and hallucinations. After I explained, the entire church leadership was called to the al-tar to lay hands on me and pray. The drumbeaters took their positions, the whirlwind team started spinning, the choir began singing and the atmosphere changed. The last time I was conscious on that altar, the choir was singing *'Ekhaya*

ezulwini kukhona izithembiso, vuma, vuma, vuma usindiswe'.
I remember feeling something huge eloping from my numb body; I suppose that is when I fell into a deep slumber.

I am not certain for how long I lay in that spiritual sedative mode. Perhaps I had also died a brief death like the Biblical Lazarus. I cannot explain what had happened to me. How could one doze off in such a noisy set up? When I woke up, I somehow felt some divine visitation, which I fail to articulate. I felt as though something was relieved from my body and soul. My body felt light again. I stood up confused as if I was struck by something. The Pastor proclaimed my healing and I was handed a small bottle of water with the instruction of sprinkling daily on my water for bathing. After the healing episode, what followed was a guilt-tripping sermon of tithing and the service ended with the congregation greeting each other outside the church building.

After the church healing incident, I never witnessed the weird dreams and visions again. I used the bottled water as instructed. From then onwards, I believed in the power of God, Moses' rod and the miracles of the whirlwind.

CHAPTER 10

Umas'hlalisane (cohabitation)

. . . .

After my moment of insanity, I was glad that my boss, Mr Peters understood my problem and took me back for my weekend job although his wife seemed displeased about it. I was doing gardening, cleaning the yard and any other masculine chore that arose in the yard or even beyond. The most pathetic part of my job was cleaning dog poop. I had grown up keeping dogs from a young age and I used to train all my dogs to poop in the bushes, not in the yard. Mr Peters' dogs were always enclosed, they were not given any chance to leave the yard unless for walks under leash. I also never understood this dog-walking act, but I had no say, it was part of my job. I was getting paid for it.

Mr Peters was Afrikaans speaking although he understood English. We never spoke much unless he was instructing me to do something. I believe he was a nice guy with a calm demeanour and had no bad blood with me. On the other hand, Mrs Peters had Obsessive Compulsive Disorder (OCD) and made my life a living hell. She complained about how I was not cleaning the yard enough, she would bark and yell every time for reasons I thought were silly.

Their yard had a huge tree that often shed its leaves and littered it with its pinkish-whitish flowers. No matter how much I would rack off the tree leaves and flowers, others would eventually fall off the tree again. There was no way that yard was going to be completely clean, according to Mrs Peters' expectations. The puppies would play with, and displace objects like shoes, children's dolls and balls in their huge yard and Mrs Peters would expect me to run after them every minute.

Mr and Mrs Peters had parallel characters; they seemed not to have anything in common. The opposites attract, people say. Mrs Peters was like cancer to anyone's flesh while her husband was as sober as a Supreme Court Judge. Every time Mrs Peters would bark at me, Mr Peters would try to calm her down in Afrikaans but she would not stop. Mr Peters appeared like a well-read man and a bookish intellectual albeit incapable of solving his household matters.

Although I understood very little Afrikaans, I could tell that the woman was toxic like garmatox even to her husband. She walked over him whenever she felt like and she seemed to interpret his politeness for a castrated man and therefore disrespected him. I wondered how they got married in the first place. Did Mr Peters fall in love with that woman sober or he was fed with love charms to blindly marry her? There was absolutely no recovery to his manhood as long as he was married to that woman. Mrs Peters was the head of the house.

I had never associated that kind of mind-blowing callousness with a White woman. In my mind, I had pictured White women as soft spoken, polite, empathetic and kind. I associated sternness and all other sorts of meanness with male figures and I was up for that. But how could a male servant react to such cold-heartedness from a woman?

When I started working for them, Mrs Peters was pregnant, so I brushed off her resentment towards me as one of those irritabilities, anger and mood swings that pregnant women often experience due to hormonal changes. I endured her eruptions until she finally gave birth. After the birth of her child, she continued and her attitude worsened even. I knew I had to look for another job.

Back at Tagwisa's house, I felt that I had overstayed my welcome. Although I had nowhere else to go, it was unheard of to live in someone else's yard without the owner knowing. My salary was not enough for me to rent my own house and if I moved to the *lok'shini,* I wouldn't afford transport costs to my work place. After working for the Peters for a while, they gave me a two months' notice that they were relocating to Cape Town. I could not follow them to Cape Town as their package was very small and the job was only for weekends. I was back to square one and unemployed. Tagwisa accommodated me nonetheless. I was also marketing for a lucrative job.

I soon received news that there was a relative searching for my whereabouts in Honeydew. Kudzani, a former primary school classmate informed me that Benkosi was in Johannesburg, Honeydew, looking for me. I wasn't sure of how I was going to react meeting my long-lost girlfriend. I was insensitive to her when I denied fathering our child at first. Even after our child was born resembling my family, I do not think I played the fatherly role, as I should have. My relationship with Benkoe was hanging, we neither re-officialised it after the pregnancy saga nor dissolved it. I was not sure if we were still in a relationship.

The day I met Benkoe in Honeydew reminded me of why I had fallen in love with her in the first place. She welcomed me with a wide smile I wasn't expecting after all I had put her through. Not only was she smiling with her mouth but her eyes too. Thank goodness, at least I was not going to start wooing her afresh.

She was wearing a drop waist dress with a huge figure belt that thinned her waist, enhanced her twins and revealed her hips. Her curves had since widened yet her waist size remained small. Why did I, in my normal senses disconnect with such a goddess? I cursed myself for not valuing the God sent woman. She was now more beautiful than ever before. My life had been barren ever since I had disconnected with her. There is something about the 'right' woman that gives life to a man but for me, I guess out of sight was out of mind. I vowed to correct my past mistakes and never let that woman go ever again. I made an instant decision to man-up.

When we met, we rekindled our love and let bygones be bygones. The question I was curious to know was how she got to South Africa. Every undocumented foreigner in South Africa always had a long story to tell about his or her journey.

Of all the dramatic and touching journeys I had heard, Benkoe's was the most unbelievable. Apparently, Benkoe and 5 other people had left their village on the 2nd of February. They alternated travelling on foot and taxi hiking at places they thought were safe enough to avoid arrest. They walked the 94km distance between Plumtree and Francistown on foot and hiked a taxi from Francistown to the border town between Botswana and South Africa. They crossed the border midnight, and decided to walk in the bushes to avoid arrest. According to her, they avoided the main road at all cost but made sure they were not far from it.

The journey took 28 days of walking in the bushes until they arrived in March. Fearing getting jailed for being illegally in the country, they were scared to even buy food at the shops. They arrived at a certain enclosed area midnight. The place was fenced and there was no other way to avoid it except going to the main road. They could not risk their lives by walking alongside the road. They decided to jump over the fence, hoping that the owners of the space were asleep since it was midnight.

The fenced area covered a huge area, and they concluded that it was probably a farm. After walking for about two kilometres into the night, lions started roaring in the vicinity. Others were roaring from the direction where they had come from, others in the surrounding area. One must diagram the kind of fright paralysis they got at that moment. While they were trying to figure out a plan, one lion marched towards them from the nearby bushes.

Women panicked and screamed their lungs out. One of the men in the group was a prophet. As the lion approached them hungrily, the prophet dug into his bag, and took his holy water and sprinkled the circumference of where they stood. To their dismay, the lion continued its journey past them without harming them. Jesus Christ! Wonders never cease to happen.

They realised in the morning that the enclosed area that they had entered midnight was actually a game reserve. If the man's holy water could shut the mouth of the lion, surely it could protect them from being arrested.

They finally arrived in Johannesburg after 28 days of travelling, sleeping and waking up in the bushes. Upon arrival in Johannesburg, Benkoe went to live with her uncle in Honeydew and eventually met other homeboys who alerted her of where I was. When we met, she was working as a florist at a nursery in Honeydew. Since I was unemployed, we decided to move in together to the room she was given at her workplace as accommodation. She was earning R65 a month and the amount was not enough to feed two adults. I was seriously looking for a job.

She eventually got another job at a tea garden and was enrolled at a bakery school. To supplement her income, she sold alcohol and cigarettes in the evening. Her goods were moving like hot cakes. Benkoe was gifted in trading. Even when we met at school, she was always selling something stretching from wild fruits, homemade sweets and snacks.

As the only unemployed man in the compound, I was awarded a patron-like position to look after the compound.

I was asked to look out for those who engaged in dangerous activities and those who sold alcohol. The irony was that I was guilty of the act in that Benkoe was involved in the alcohol selling business.

Benkoe sold cold castle lager and beer even though we did not own a fridge. She bought ice blocks daily to cool the alcohol. Her alcohol was always preferred by buyers as her competitors' stock was not as cold. The business earned her the title *maSeven*, who sold ice-cold beer. She also sold *nkaw'za* (cigarettes) in different types. The danger to that business was that smokers would knock even midnight when they were cigar-thirsty. They could not contain their cigarette cravings; hence, they knocked any time of the night.

Although we were in desperate need of money, these midnight knocks irritated us. So, to benefit from the irritation, we put up a poster written, "After 20:30 pm, the cigarette costs R0.20c higher than the normal price." Customers had to pay for the inconvenience they caused.

Benkoe fell pregnant. I don't know how she fell pregnant as I was under the impression that she was on contraceptives. Considering my financial status, I was not ready for a second child. Sometimes women intentionally fall pregnant to corner a man to marry them especially since we already had a child together. I wasn't sure if I was cornered or indeed the contraception malfunctioned. What was weird about her pregnancy was that it loved another man, Stephen. Stephen was a photographer from Tsholotsho who lived across our street. He was very good at his job. He could edit one's picture to be anything requested. He could easily edit a person's picture and place it in an eggshell or anything creative. He could edit one's complexion or edit women's pictures to have the coca-cola bottle figures they always desired. For that reason, all women loved Stephen, even Abelungu. Women generally love looking fake, they love what they are not. They adored Stephen as he had the ability to exaggerate how they looked.

Men disliked Stephen, for he sought too much of their women's attention. When Benkoe fell pregnant, she would ask me to accompany her to visit Stephen. I was often told that pregnancy could make a woman behave weirdly, but I failed to fathom this behaviour. I wasn't sure whether I should refuse or not. If she was seeing Stephen would she, in her normal senses ask me to escort her to visit him? At the same time, I low key thought that they were secretly dating.

I decided to give her the benefit of doubt and would escort her to visit Stephen. Perhaps it was one of those mysteries of pregnancies that men would never understand. Whenever we got to Stephen's place, she would greet him and demand that we go back home after two minutes. This became a routine and I soon awarded myself some peace that this was certainly one of those obscurities of pregnancy.

Benkoe soon gave birth to a bouncing baby girl. After giving birth, she stopped the Stephen-trips and we laughed about it every time the matter arose. She also could not believe herself and she appreciated my understanding of that abnormality.

Although children were always a blessing, we could not afford our own lives, let alone a child. My girlfriend was the only one with an income. The caretaker job awarded me peanuts, only enough to buy relish and nothing more. The kind of job she had did not award maternity leave. She worked even on the day she gave birth. The ambulance picked her up from her workplace to the hospital.

Other than not affording to have a child at that time, it was taboo to impregnate a girl twice without paying lobola for her. It was an insult to her family. I had to do something. I had to man up. Benkoe and I were both undocumented foreigners in the country and had also borne an undocumented child. I could imagine a jail sentence with a child. The thought was sickening.

When our daughter was born. I had to rethink what I was taught with regards to being a man. I watched Benkoe struggle to juggle between work and taking care of the child, doing laundry and changing nappies. I failed to locate my role in all this as an African man. I started helping changing nappies and bathing the baby although I often felt like a castrated man. In urban spaces gender roles don't remain constant like in the villages, they are constantly amended as circumstances are always different. I had no choice but to help my girlfriend. She was employed and I wasn't. She provided for my wellbeing, so I had to be useful where I could.

After our child was born, Benkoe's employer started dodging paying their salaries. There were rumours that he was planning to relocate to England. Upon confronting her employer about her unpaid salary, Benkoe lost her job. The employer indicated that he was doing her a favour by employing her when she had a baby whom she often brought to the workplace. The breaks she would take to breastfeed the baby were negating the company and reducing productivity.

CHAPTER 11

An unfriendly neighbour

After the birth of our child, we were evacuated from the backroom we were renting. The landlord was annoyed by my child who would yell non-stop, day and night. We got another apartment that had a communal toilet we shared with other tenants. Each tenant rented one small room, which served many purposes. One corner of the room was a kitchen, the other a bathroom and the rest of the room was a bedroom.

Our ever-crying child annoyed neighbours, although others tolerated and sympathised with us as they were parents too, there was one particular tenant who rejoiced at our demise.

A Pedi woman rented the room adjacent to ours. I never got to know her name, we called her Mam'Pedi. She stayed alone most of the times and her partner only visited on weekends. The woman was very mean to us, xenophobic and very prickly. Whenever my child slept, she would turn on her radio full blast and the baby would wake up and wail again.

We shared one electricity metre box as tenants. There were always quarrels over how much each tenant should contribute. She would count occupants of each household and expect every member of the household, even a one-month-old baby to contribute. When other tenants raised the matter of her partner who visited every weekend to contribute a certain percentage too, hell broke loose. Other tenants spoke Tshivenda and Tsonga and Mam'Pedi decided to consciously paint them as foreigners too because of the complexity of their languages and their darker skin.

Mam'Pedi would utter xenophobic sentiments to us all whenever we tried to negotiate things like the electricity bill, cleaning of the communal toilet and the yard.

Women took turns in cleaning the toilet and sweeping the yard. When it was other people's turn, Mam'Pedi would sweep off the dirt from her own room and leave it to be blown by the wind and mess the entire yard. How could a woman be so thorough in punishing another? Mam'Pedi was vindictive and provocative to the bone as she was always looking for any opportunity there was, to drive others to the verge of insanity. She was a thorn and always ensnaring everyone into picking a fight with her.

CHAPTER 12

Own home

. . . .

With no form of employment and our child undocumented, we decided to go back home, refresh and think straight about our future. Home, no matter how it is, no matter how it looks, it is a place where one can feed on positive energy. It is where one's umbilical cord is buried; it is where one's roots are. No matter how appalling conditions can be at home, it is unforgettable. The bigger plan was to build our own home.

The beauty of the village life is that it did not require a lot of money as long as there was enough seasonal rainfall, people survived and people supported each other. A lot of things were done communally like building. Neighbours shared their grains of crops, beans, dried relish with those starting new families. Others would go as far as giving cows, goats, sheep and chicken to start off a family with.

The journey back home was an uphill struggle because of immigration procedures for an undocumented family. Although we were busted several times by immigrant officers, they let us go since we were going back home. There was absolutely no point in arresting an undocumented person going back to his or her country.

Since I was not married to Benkoe, it was taboo for me to take her to my people even if we had two children together. Upon arrival, Benkoe went to her own people with the baby and I went to mine.

Gogo had become frailer and could not live by herself. Her cousin had since taken her in, in the same village. As a result, she left home, which was in ruins when we arrived. That made me realise how long I had been in South Africa without means of communicating and checking up on Gogo. I was left with no choice but to temporarily reside at the cousin's home.

After two weeks in the village, I sent my people to Benkoe's village for lobola negotiations. I did not have much except a few goats that I was given by Gogo. I was confident that the in-laws would not object as their daughter already had two children by me. Therefore, refusing my offer and hand in marriage meant that their daughter stood higher chances of not getting married in future. In my culture, one does not complete paying lobola. Lobola is paid in instalments as a sign of respect to the in-laws. Paying the entire amount charged at once shows pompousness and lack of humility. It simply tells the family that you perceive their daughter as extremely affordable that you can pay for her at one go. Prolonging the instalments means that their daughter is a jewel that you cannot afford to pay for at once.

After the lobola negotiations and the payment of the first instalment, Benkoe officially became my wife and she came to stay with us. Life became unbearable staying with our extended family. We were reduced to children who would be sent to run around and do errands. I was a married man but I was reduced to a small boy under another man's roof. I also did not like how Gogo was disrespected even by children. I was grateful for their gesture of accommodating her in my absence, but my heart wept every time I saw children poking her and adults doing nothing about it. I had to do something as a man.

One evening we were sitting around the glowing fire in the thatched kitchen when my cousin served us the evening meal. The family was extremely huge with our teenage cousins either pregnant or having small children. It was almost impossible to find a pot big enough to cook a meal enough for everyone. Each day, there had to be one person who went to bed with their tummy half full. As we ate, Gogo asked if there weren't any left overs in the pot. The response was *'mungabhuzwa benyu bana, kana imwi mozwala banotebela hhango besingazibe kuti modlani'*. This loosely translates to 'you should ask your own children who are scattered all over the world but cannot remember that you need food'. I was hit below the belt and I immediately lost my appetite. If such a statement could be verbalised, it means it had been a bottled and ticking time bomb for a long time. Gogo was not the only targeted hearer, I was too. Gogo and my small family had certainly overstayed our welcome in that home. A million shreds of pain stuck within me and I felt emotionally handicapped. At that moment, I knew I had to do something.

We all retired to bed. My wife and baby quietly lay on the bed next to me. As soon as we extinguished the last candle, it was I, head-on with my thoughts. The night was terrifyingly and spooky silent. It was so dark that I was looking into nothingness. I descended into my mind, trying to squeeze my eyes shut, but my mind was wide-awake. I heard a pronounced voice whispering in my ears, saying "it's time to be a man". I could not distinguish whether it was my inner voice speaking to me, the Holy Spirit or someone else. I was not sure of how the Holy Spirit speaks to someone, although I had constantly asked Pastors and deacons that question. The answers always varied and sounded unsatisfactory. Now, how could I be a man when no man taught me to be one? I travelled into a locomotive train of thought. Stopped at several stations, boarded again, trying to find myself.

The night was as stony silent as death. I was rescued from my own thoughts by a musically buzzing mosquito. Eventually, I could hear the faint and strange honking sounds of dogs from a distance, the hooting and shrieking sounds of night owls, the croaking sounds of frogs and toads, chirping crickets, the sounds of howling hyenas vulturing on vulnerable animals of the wild and the giggle-like sounds made by jackals after catching prey or repelling intruders. In my village, humans and animals co-existed, the former ruled by day and the latter by night.

It was a restless night for me. Every time I closed my eyes, the images of my little family's faces haunted me. Their pretty faces didn't mirror the turmoil in my soul. Their soft snores and idyllic slumber was soothing, I knew I had to do them right. I decided that night, that the following day I was going to leave and build my own home. I imagined how drastically my life would change, for either the best or worst. What if I failed to stand on my own two feet? How was I to sustain a home without any form of employment? Despite these rhetoric questions, I had made up my mind. There was no turning back, I felt ready for what awaited me, either good or bad.

As soon as the first cocks crew, I woke my wife up and told her about my plan to leave and start our own home. She was confused by my impulsiveness. She suggested that we wait a bit and follow a proper channel of informing and consulting the elders. I was tired of being treated like a child when I could be a man. My wife insisted that at least we do the honour of respecting elders and sit them down although on a short notice. We agreed that we were going to inform them midday and start the following day.

I went to scout the site adjacent to Gogo's home, where we were residing before I left for South Africa. I placed four pegs on the marked area where the yard was going to be. As customary, I went to inform the chief that I had spotted land where I wanted to build my children a home. The chief did not object as the place was within the area where my ancestors resided. The chief gave me his blessings and wished me well.

It is also custom in the village that one notifies potential neighbours about his/her intentions of starting a home. The traditional way of informing them is to say, 'If you see fire at night, do not panic and think its spooks and ghosts, it is my home'. I notified all neighbours and then went home to break the news. The elders were not happy with my sudden decision; they felt that I was undermining their authority by not informing them of my plans timeously since I was living under their roof. I apologised for my impulsiveness but had to carry on with my plan.

In my village, when one decided to start a home, they could not return back to their former even to sleep. They had to continue with what they started. I shepherded my little family and we left for our newly pegged ground with no structure whatsoever. The day we left, we had young men and women in the village who assisted with weeding the yard while others helped with a temporal structure made of tree branches for sleeping at night. Such structures were dangerous as they could harbour dangerous snakes and scorpions. We had a young baby but had no choice but to sleep in that structure.

Within two weeks, one hut was complete and that gave our home dignity. Although we started our home without anything, not even a single pot or spoon, community members came in handy and they assisted even beyond our expectations. On the third week, the second hut was almost complete. I was humbled by this humanness of people in my village. I had long lost any form of connection with them since I was in South Africa for a long time, but that did not stop their humanity towards me. I am forever grateful.

My wife worked magic to make the home a home. She decorated the huts with clay paintings and made mud shelves in the kitchen for easy storage of utensils.

When the second house was complete, we fetched Gogo to stay with us. News soon travelled that I had built a home. Mother also visited to pay her respects to the new home and congratulate me. We also fetched our first-born daughter from her maternal family to complete the family. Finally, my family was coming together. I looked back to the story of my life and could not believe that I had a home to call my own, I had a complete family. My children were to grow up knowing the love of both their parents. I was tearful. My life changed; I became a man.

Although for once in my life I had mother, Gogo, wife and my two children in one home, another unanticipated problem arose. I was facing a life-draining situation of having to constantly choose between mother and the mother of my children. The two Alpha females were competing for my attention, always at war with each other, each reporting to me and expecting me to be the adjudicator every time they quarrelled.

I was never ready for this hotspot that I found myself in. Although I loved my wife dearly, I was also trying to create a relationship with the mother that I never had in my childhood. She was absent most of the times.

Although mother was absent when I married my wife, the moment she saw her, she did not really like her demeanour and she resented that I had not married a fellow Kalanga but a Ndebele instead. On the other hand, my wife was a different kind of woman, she also did not even try to purchase love from her in-laws as most women do when their marriages are still fresh.

In the society I grew up in, when a woman marries a man, she also marries his family including his mother. Thus, she has to learn to manoeuvre and tiptoe her way into his family cautiously without treading on anyone's corns. However, my wife was disqualified even before she could enter the marriage. She would not stoop to that kind of treatment and it often embarrassed me from my family. She was considered arrogant although she did nothing wrong except standing up for herself to defeat the ill-treatment of newly married women.

The frequent feuds between mother and my wife escalated one day when I was away. Apparently, they were having breakfast; tea and bread with peanut butter.

Mother said to my wife, 'I see that you can actually plaster a four roomed house and finish it on your own'.

Wifey: 'Why do you say that?'

Mother: 'I see the way you butter your slices of bread with peanut butter. You do it so skilfully without leaving any patch unbuttered'.

As soon as I entered the homestead, my wife could not wait for me to sit down to report what mother had said to her. God forbid! That was an extreme sense of callousness clothed like a joke. This incident made me feel *ding-dong*, I was immersed with shock and unease. The two women were driving me to the verge of insanity. How could elderly people be so prickly towards each other like children? Despite the awkward position I was in, both women expected me to be the umpire of their drama.

It did not take a rocket scientist to figure out that Benkoe was extremely angry. Her face showed helplessness as she stood before me in a daze, not daring to move. This signified to me that she was tired of the verbal war with mother. Although I was drained by the rivalry between two important women in my life, I had to sit them down and address whatever differences they had. I believed in the adage that matters had to be settled and the truth must be told no matter who it hurts. I had no choice but address the elephant in the room.

Upon sitting them down, drama hung in the air like clouds. I could tell from mother's meandering speech that in her defence, she was not telling the truth. Her side of the story that her daughter in-law poked her first was too farfetched to be true. She blamed her for overdramatizing a lame issue. My wife on the other hand, although I was certain that she was also not a saint, she was very careful with her speech. Everything she said was always calculated and left mother feeling somewhat imprudent.

Mother's brewing anger exploded and reached its peak like melting lava. She dramatically wept and played victim in the whole saga. Although I did my best to settle the *makoti* (daughter in-law) /*mamazala* (mother in-law) rivalry, mother packed her bags and departed the following morning. She said she could not stand being disrespected by *umuntu wokuza* (a trespasser). I felt helpless. I had failed to solve their feuding. But maybe I had done my best. After all, I had never heard of any makoti who got along with her mother in-law. The two women always competed for attention from this central figure trying to unite them. Perhaps this tension was inevitable after all and beyond fix. When we woke up the following morning, mother's existence had vanished into thin air.

After a week, I left home for Johannesburg to continue with my job-hunting expedition. This time around, I was never arrested on the road, even upon arrival. My wife had to take care of our children and Gogo. A few months after I had left, I received news that Gogo was seriously ill and could not do anything for herself. My wife took care of her. She fed her and bathed her.

It's tough being a woman, it's tough being a daughter in law. Would a man take care of his in-laws like that? Especially when the relationship was that fresh. They barely had a connection to the extent of having the patience to nurse a person who could not even eat by herself or go to the restroom by herself. Women are just super beings; their motherly nature is sometimes beyond comprehension.

Gogo passed on after two months of being bedridden. Although death could never sit well with anyone, she was old and had been tortured by her sickness. I was at peace that she finally rested; her death was better off than the pain she experienced in the latter days of her life. I had received a telegram when she became gravely ill and I went to be with her during her last days. She departed in my arms. After her burial, I went back to Johannesburg.

A few years later, my father passed on. I was grateful that although we never had a strong father-son bond, we communicated and I visited him occasionally when I got a chance. After his passing, we created a bond with my siblings to undo the wrongs of our parents. The aim was for our children to grow up knowing each other.

In the year 2010, I lost mother. I would forever regret that I failed to burry my own mother. Border laws were strict and my passport had expired, so I was waiting for the outcome of my passport when mother passed on. Burials back home took place within few days of one's passing, even if I was to organise an emergency passport, I would have received it way after her burial. I had outgrown the stage of border jumping. Although this was a tough decision to make, my relatives judged me for not burying my mother. However, it was impossible for them to make moral judgement without taking a trip in my shoes. As soon as I got my passport, I went to cast a stone on mother's grave and uttered my send off. REST IN PEACE MOTHER.

CHAPTER 13

God is Able Christian Ministries

My neighbour, a devout Christian invited me to a Pentecostal church called God is Able Christian Ministries. I had heard so many stories about Pentecostal churches regarding their sudden mushrooming and overtaking the Christian religion with modern ways of worship, speaking in tongues, modern dressing and dancing. I was sceptical about attending, but I did nonetheless.

I enjoyed the service, from the preaching to praise and worship. The Pastor was preaching in a civil manner, things seemed orderly compared to my encounter in Zion. People were dressed formally, men in suits and women in high heels. Everybody looked highly esteemed and very respectful. Although the congregation comprised of people of different ethnic groups, most people spoke isiXhosa. The Senior Pastor was Xhosa, I guess he drew Xhosa followers as a result.

The Pastor however preached in English although an interpreter interpreted in isiXhosa to accommodate the wider audience who perhaps could not understand the Queen's language. The beauty about Nguni languages such as isiNdebele which I speak, isiXhosa, isiZulu and isiSwati is that they are closely related and hence easy to understand. Although I understood isiXhosa, there were words that were new to me, whose pronunciation fascinated me such as *uxanduva* (responsibility), *ukubhidisa umtyoli* (confusing the enemy) and *krakra* (bitterness). I was amused by the sound produced by the interpreter as her lower and upper jaws sandwiched her tongue. I tried but failed to imitate it soundly.

I was new to the concept of tithing. Although I had heard of it before at the Zion Church, it was not explained fully. When it was time for tithe and offering, the lady who sat next to me counted a huge sum of R50 and R100 notes, enveloped them and took them upfront. I was wide-eyed. I had never imagined such a huge amount of money being given to the church just like that. I soon learnt that the lady was well known for being a Kingdom financier. She paid tithe and gave offering faithfully such that she would be referred to as exemplary occasionally when money issues arose in church.

Such rare people would be awarded too much respect in church and they enjoyed it. Whenever the church fell into a financial crisis, everyone knew the lady would rescue it. That elevated her status such that she earned more respect than the senior Pastor himself. She was able to make decisions for the church without objection and contestation from anyone. It was her money that finally defeated the patriarchal organisation of the church.

I enjoyed the service though there were things I failed to comprehend, such as the eating of biscuits and the drinking of red grapetiser. My neighbour, Nkosi, explained to me that it was the Holy Communion. He said the biscuit represented the bread, symbolising the body of Christ that was wounded for our transgressions. The grapetiser juice represented the wine, symbolising the blood of Jesus that was shed on the cross. I didn't ask further, fearing to expose my ignorance of Christian matters.

I became a loyal member of God is Able Christian Ministries. After about three months of attending church, I fell for the tithe gospel. The concept of tithing was preached almost on a daily basis and I started faithfully paying my tithe only because I was scared of the consequences thereof. It was preached in church that billionaires were blessed because they were faithful in paying tithes. The more I listened and became conscious of the tithe gospel, the more I began to see the consequences of not paying tithe regularly.

In the months I omitted paying tithe, I would strangely fail to account how I spent my money or just had many emergencies that needed money. So, I concluded that not paying tithe was taboo in my world though other people prospered all the same without paying tithe, it was strange, I thought. I was confused. I did not know how God operated.

My commitment in church was soon visible and I joined the Men's Ministry where we advised the youth about marriage and courtship. However, there were times I would go to church out of routine, just to clear my conscience. Not going to church meant facing strange expressions from fellow churchgoers during the week, the ones that silently said you have become a heathen and you need the Holy Spirit.

I would therefore, out of duty, go to church, although I would occasionally miss the entire sermon. I would be present, yet so far away. The silence of the congregants and the voice of the preacher would create a conducive environment and award me somewhat solitary moments to think about a lot of things; to think about my bank balance, to think about my wife, sex and anything that amused me. In the process, I would constantly recollect myself and remind myself that I was in church; hence, I had to listen to the sermon only to discover that it was a guilt-inducing sermon about serving in church, tithing, attending week services or fornication. Fornication was a topic we were all scared of, especially when the preacher said people fornicate in their thoughts. I was also guilty of missing intercession; I was guilty of arriving two hours into the service. Although a faithful member of the church, I felt I was distant from God.

The church had huge clocks on all its four walls, ironically, we never dismissed on time. During one service, I glanced at the clock; it was 12:30pm. I was glad that the service was almost over. I was anticipating that we soon say 'grace' inharmoniously like crèche-going infants as we usually did when closing the service. The preacher summoned those who had their tithes and offerings to the front. I had paid my tithe using cell phone banking as previously encouraged by the church leadership. I resented the long walk from my back seat to pay my tithe at the front. As if that was all, I resented the idea that money was being counted by people I did not want to know how much I earned.

I rebuked my awkward thoughts, re-summoned myself from the wicked thoughts in church. After the tithe-offering roll call, it was time for announcements, yes, I was glad the service was finally almost over. The third announcement read, "This is to remind you that we are hosting our annual conference next week, if you have not contributed your R50 fee, please do so at the church office in town by Wednesday. Apostle Khumalo will be the main speaker, so come expectant". The last announcement read, "All the sons and daughters of God is Able Christian Ministries remain behind".

I did not know what the announcement meant, was it a trap? Who was a son, who was not? Who was a daughter and who was not? I did not know what I was. I was stuck between going out of church and remaining behind. I contemplated. Leaving was my first choice, but then I thought that the Pastor would be hurt when I decided I was not a son. I thought to myself that I would not blame myself for such an ambiguous statement. I decided to sit and become a son.

What followed was another guilt-inducing sermon of how the sons and daughters had neglected the church, how they miss intercession, how they came late and how the church was dirty. The meeting ended when all the sons and daughters picked duties in preparation for next week's conference. My duty was to contribute cash that was to buy the floor polish and bathroom cleaning products. I liked them, at least they did not require me to be in church at 07:30am on Sunday, nor did they require me to stand before the congregation at any point.

I contemplated going to church the following Sunday. I thought of the ground-breaking sermon to be delivered by Apostle Khumalo. He was a good preacher; his interpretation of the Bible was always extraordinary. I knew him from the previous conference held in the church. His sermon was awakening; it lifted my spirit when I doubted the existence of God.

I wondered in my thoughts what an Apostle was, what was the difference between an Apostle and a Pastor? I was ignorant, but I preferred to remain like that. As a senior church citizen, it was odd not to know such things. I knew that by enquiring from fellow Christians, I would get a scripture quotation from Hebrews 5:13-14 which talks about Christians still drinking milk when they are supposed to be at a stage of eating solid food. I was that Christian.

There was just another concern about the coming of Pastor Khumalo that excited and scared me at the same time. By the end of his sermon, he would make us pledge huge sums of money to the church, I recalled from my previous encounter. But he did not force anyone, we pledged on our own, perhaps it was the move of the Holy Spirit. If it was not a force matter, why was I scared? I asked myself.

Every time when there was a visiting Pastor/Apostle, whatever the difference, they would either preach about finance, taking care of the Pastor or serving in church. I wondered if the resident Pastor would have had a brief meeting with the visiting one to discuss what his congregation needed to hear, or it was the Holy Spirit showing the visiting Pastor/Apostle what to preach about. I was confused.

After a series of contemplations, I decided that I needed a spiritual revival; hence, I went to church. The Apostle's sermon would leave me bubbling with fresh optimism. He had a highly imagistic biblical vocabulary that I adored. As discussed last week at the sons and daughters meeting, we were to be in church by 08:30 to ensure all was in order in the house of God. We had to impress Apostle Khumalo. His church back in the Mpumalanga province was a double storey-like auditorium setup. It was a warm place to be, it was like a hotel. Who would not want to be in a place like that? "That is why he had a congregation of more than 500 people every Sunday yet we were a small intimate church with about 70 people", I thought to myself. We worshiped in a huge building, formerly a pen fattening shelter that had been enclosed with common bricks on the sides upon redirecting the purpose of the building.

I arrived in church at 09:30 am. It was intercession time. Brother Isaac led intercession in what appeared like mini-sermons coupled with altar calls and prayer breaks in between. I sat down and closed my eyes as the prayer point was that of binding the strong man (demons) according to the book Prayer Rain by a Nigerian author Dr Olukoye that we often used as a spiritual warfare manual.

Soon after the prayer point, Brother Isaac spoke about how Christians were unable to defeat the enemy. It was because they could not speak in tongues. "Tongues are a language understood by God only, a language that silences and confuses the enemy", he raised his voice and thundered in a theatrical way. He made an altar call of those who could not speak in tongues. I did not know whether I was able to speak in tongues or not, I had not tried. I preferred listening to myself when I talked to God; hence, I prayed in the language I understood.

Trying to speak in tongues was awkward for me; it was like learning to become left-handed at old age. It felt unnecessary and scary. I was scared of insulting God in an unknown language. What if satan intercepted my prayer, took over and insulted God? No no no! I could not risk offending God. I was self-cautious. I always had a desperate desire to try but I was demotivated when I attended a church service and one of the prayerful sisters prayed in tongues at the altar call and the guest Prophetess said the tongues were from a wrong source. I was sceptical and uneasy.

I did not want to embarrass myself; hence I did not go to the altar call. I watched anxiously how the people upfront would receive the spirit of speaking in tongues. I told myself that, I was in the same building, so I would also receive tongues without embarrassing myself up front. I would not miss the Holy Spirit's divine visitation in the same building, never! The saints who 'could' speak in tongues started moving up and down the building, speaking in tongues. I stood up, followed suit, diplomatically blending in like a chameleon. Kalanga was the only 'unknown tongue' in the building, so I also started confusing the enemy ..."*Ndzimu tate, Ndzimu nkololo wakafa ekamuka...*" At the altar call, brother Isaac prayed for those who could not speak in tongues individually and then ordered each one of them to start praying in tongues as they stood there. Jesus Christ!

Brother Isaac was very pompous in his Christianity; he was not hesitant to ridicule baby Christians in order to elevate his spiritual status in the eyes of the larger congregation, hence some members of the church always received him with disdain. We secretly called him Deputy-Pastor. It was clear he was campaigning for the Pastoral position yet the Pastor would constantly omit him in his yearly ordinations of junior Pastors.

Intercession was followed by praise and worship, which we all enjoyed. It was soon partially interrupted by the grand entrance of our senior Pastor, the visiting Apostle and his wife, a lady-usher carrying Bibles, note books and tablets, which I assumed belonged to the first trio, and a bouncer like brother whom I assumed was the Apostle's body guard, or maybe he was just a church brother accompanying his Apostle. Our senior Pastor reported to the pulpit, took an extra mic and began mimicking the song in a tune that went parallel to the one the lead singer led. We concealed our discomfiture and continued singing. As the song halted, our Pastor introduced his friend and invited him to the pulpit.

The visiting Apostle was a potbellied baobab looking man, with skin the colour of dark chocolate. His huge smile revealed his yellow incisors and canines the size of piano keys. His light blue shirt could not adequately tuck his protruding belly. He started sweating before preaching. I gazed at him and his wife, back and forth. She was a finely sculptured woman with an hourglass figure. They were an imperfect match physically. I tried to picture their intimacy. It was unthinkable. I quickly rebuked my wayward thoughts and listened to the man of God. He started by greeting the church and introduced the bone of his bones, flesh of his flesh, his wife. Within few seconds, I had returned to my wayward train of thoughts. I wondered if the wife's appraisal was real. Most Pastors/Apostles seemed to have the Romeo and Juliet kind of affection. Maybe their marriages were sanctified by default, or the statement was just a habitual icebreaker. I re-summoned myself again and made a small repentance prayer.

The sermon was on the Abrahamic faith. It was a touching sermon; one that could not be easily forgotten. The Apostle was screaming noisily, no one could afford to doze off that day. I did not look at the clock that day; I was enjoying the sermon, absorbed into the word of God. As the sermon came to a conclusion, the Apostle linked the sermon to giving your last possession, while having faith in God. He talked of the sacrificial offering of faith, the kind of offering that Abraham was about to do with Isaac had God not provided the sacrificial animal at the last minute. He finally concluded the sermon by asking ushers to bring offering baskets up front.

He called for people to give like they had never given before. People stood up to give. The Apostle emptied the offering baskets on the floor to unveil how much people had given. The finance treasurer was soon called to count the money. It was R579.90. The Apostle lamented how the whole church could give such a small amount of money and cited that it was a shame that there were people still offering cents. A second offering was called as people were asked to do better as the church needed electricity, the church's water bills had to be paid, church transport needed fuel. That amount could not pay all those bills. We enjoyed being ferried by the church combi from bus stops but had never imagined that it used fuel like any other car. That was a disturbing reality.

People offered again in the second offering and the amount rose to +R2000. I did not carry any money to church that day, in fact, I felt my tithe was big enough and I doubted if God would punish me for not offering in church. After the second offering, the Apostle asked for pledges from those who did not have money at that moment but had the Abrahamic faith that they would soon have money. People wrote their pledges on papers and put in the offering baskets. They had to indicate how much they were to pay per month and for how long. As I thought that was the conclusion to the offering crescendo, more was coming.

The Apostle requested all those who were employed to stand on their feet. The whole church gazed at each other in a state of confusion. We were all trying to stomach the statement. At that point, I wished I was not employed. We knew each other;

we knew who was employed and who was not. While we remained diplomatically quiet and in a state of hesitation, "I mean all those with payslips and even those who get paid via envelopes", the Apostle elaborated with the depth of his voice intensifying. I could not dodge this roll call; everyone knew I was employed, so I stood up. All those employed stood up.

The Apostle with his mic went to each one of us to ask how much we would pledge per month. We had to announce to the whole church, to make a covenant to the whole church. Others pledged big moneys, R1000, R500 and it was my turn. I honestly did not want to pledge, I had many financial commitments, I had school going children and commitments back home. After all, I faithfully paid tithe, so God would understand, I thought. I pledged R50 per month. The Apostle did not request the congregation to clap hands for my pledge as he routinely did to others, instead he cleared his throat and echoed, "Church listen to me" he pitched up his voice, "God will reward you in the same measure you give Him". My legs dissolved below me, I sat and sank into my seat, strongly defeated and crushed inside.

CHAPTER 14

Joblessness and living

The sun cut itself through the small opening of my shack on a Thursday morning. The weather outside was serene, the sky was empty, even the birds had recoiled into hallow spaces of nature. How could a person sleep until the sun's rays torch their buttocks? Those were Gogo's favourite words when we were growing up.

Oops! It was my court date. The thought of it was energy zapping. Where did I get the guts to take Umlungu to court? I felt like this was the beginning of a horror movie in my life. I was caught up in a dual consciousness; a back and forth-mental chess, to let it go or not. I was hopelessly optimistic about the outcome.

I took a taxi and reported to the labour court in Johannesburg to try to undo the damage done to my future. At the entrance, I met my representatives who gave me a short briefing. Although I had been to court before, the seriousness of the atmosphere sent shivers to my spine. It was not for people like me with a speech disability. I prayed that I would not have to speak; otherwise, my teeth would bite my tongue in the process and things would go south.

The court lingo was fascinating though. All those who got a chance to speak, spoke in a manner that proved that they were trained with thoroughness to qualify for their jobs and had excellent rhetorical gymnastics. I was certain that the way people addressed the Judge was the same way we would address God when we get to Heaven. His level of authority in court seemed unparalleled.

The presiding officer, a man whose role was said to restore the livelihood of others introduced himself, introduced the matter and asked for my name and the name of my opponent. Mr Botha's representative stated that his client was sick and had therefore absented himself. The matter was therefore postponed and an agreed date was set.

Just like that, the day was a wasted one. How does the system work kanti? Why would they allow us to waste transport money and go to court only to be told that we could not carry on due to the absence of one person? I could not understand how the justice system worked. It had failed me. Every Rand counts for an unemployed man. A taxi fare to Johannesburg city and back was equivalent a loaf of bread, a menu for two days.

The second court date finally arrived. I was not as nervous as on the first. At least I had an idea of the court environment and the mannerisms thereof. To my dismay, Mr Botha's legal representative argued that summons had not been properly served to his client. Thus, the matter was postponed again on a technicality that my Scorpion Legal representatives were supposed to take care of. Most of these terminologies were beyond my comprehension although my representatives, Scorpion Legal, explained in the local Zulu language. As disappointed as I was, life had to carry on. I somehow got accustomed to the nothingness that this court offered me.

Another date was pronounced and this time I prayed that God or my ancestors; either of the two would assist in concluding the matter to my advantage. Had I had enough money for transport, I would go back to Zion church that healed me from the mysterious hallucinations and hauntings, whatever that was. I was certain that the court case was nothing before the Zionists if they could heal the madness that befell me some time ago. God is Able Christian Ministries had relocated to Tembisa; I could not afford the transport costs to go to church every Sunday. Perhaps my non-attendance at church and putting to halt my tithe payment had resulted in the situation that I was in. When the third court day arrived, Mr Botha was nowhere to be found. He was declared sick and proof of his illness was evidenced.

These people were testing my patience and playing hide and seek games with my emotions. I was sick, sick, sick and tired of their nonsense. With an empty pocket and an empty stomach, how was l going to afford another trip to a blinded court, a court whose rules were determined by the offender. I knew my fate was sealed, closed and slammed like a door.

This whole saga began on a lazy Saturday in the Randburg CBD when I was doing my weekend errands, buying groceries and window-shopping. A group of energetic young people in black pants and red tops stopped me. They had red and black fliers that they were handing to people and seemed to be advertising some invisible product. I was not interested in what they were selling, I usually did not pay attention to street vendors no matter how good-looking or eloquent they were. I was not the kind of person who buys invisible products sold through fliers. I thought they were fake and were a rip-off of some sort.

Out of politeness, I decided to stop and lend them an ear. They were selling a Scorpion Legal Protection cover. I had never really thought I would be in any legal trouble in South Africa. The only trouble I had with the law was being an illegal and undocumented citizen. I had since applied for a passport and a work permit. After five years of obtaining a work permit, I applied for a permanent resident permit, which I obtained. Thus, I was now legal in the country and a law-abiding resident.

The presence of two White ladies amongst the group assured me of the authenticity of whatever they were selling. I had not heard of Abelungu defrauding people before on the streets except big things like the land and mines. This service must be legit; I assured myself and dropped my gut. They explained how no one was immune to false-accusation or how one could find him/herself in trouble unknowingly. They also clarified how Scorpion Legal Protection Cover operates, with the lowest premium being R49.99.

I am not sure if I was convinced enough, or I just failed to find words to decline the offer. I did the paperwork, and that is how I became a Scorpion member, forking out R49.99 monthly. Little did I know that the scorpion cover was leading me into a ditch.

At the time, I was residing at Kya Sands. I had mounted my own shack and my cost of living was very low. At least I was not paying any rent. The only significant amount I had to set aside monthly other than groceries and supporting my wife and children back home, was my transport fee, to and fro work. My boss Mr Botha, whom I worked for as a 'garden boy' was residing in the heart of Randburg. When I signed the Scorpion legal membership documents, I put Mr Botha's address, as it was the most reliable. I had never seen any mail being delivered at the shacks where I stayed.

Scorpion sent mails every month and Mrs Botha was kind enough to hand them to me sealed as they came. After about 6 months of receiving the Scorpion mail and working as hard as I could to keep the Botha's yard clean, I arrived at the work place only to be received with tension in the house. I failed to read what was going on, the Bothas seemed to push each other to break the news. My adrenaline started pumping. None of them seemed brave enough to hit the snake in the head, but eventually the wife told me that they could not afford to pay me anymore, so they decided to let me go with immediate effect. My entire body sunk. I had children at a boarding school back home, how was I to pay their school fees? What was I to tell my wife? I had projects at home and I was extending my main house. All this needed money to be completed. I began to see my life taking a twist for the worst. My children's dreams were being aborted in a split second.

I asked about our initial verbal agreement of giving each other a one-month notice in my strong and dense Kalanga accented English. They looked at each other as if to say they could not imagine me questioning my terms of employment. I had portrayed myself as the 'yes Baas' kind of employee incapable of questioning anything my employer said.

I suppose they had not really planned how they were to get rid of me. Mrs Botha tried to explain economics that I did not understand of the fiscal policy of the country, the losing value of the Rand and so forth and how it affected their own savings what what. I did not understand a dime of what she said, but I assume she was using big words to silence me. Before she could finish, Mr Botha perhaps read my face and realised that I did not understand anything and dropped a bombshell. He burst from nowhere and said to his wife, 'why are you meandering? won't you address the Scorpion matter?'

Oops, Mr Botha was not calculative at all and very clumsy with words. How could he mention that? That was the expression I got from his wife. She seemed hesitant to talk about the Scorpion matter. She handed me the Scorpion letter, which was open and told me plain that the family was not happy with me being a Scorpion member, but she emphasised that, that was not the reason why they were dismissing me. Mrs Botha had a tactical mind compared to her husband, but I was not moved by her lame explanation. Mr Botha said they were giving me the month' salary although it was mid-month.

I had mixed emotions and felt that arguing with the Bothas would not help. I had outgrown my usefulness in their home and joining Scorpion was a threat to them. The whole incident felt like a form of some divine force issuing me with a punishment. I ran out of words and tuck my tail between my legs as I exited the Bothas' yard. As I took a taxi home, I began introspecting my life, thinking about whom I had wronged and imagining who could have a grudge with me to inflict so much pain to my life. The dismissal was definitely a spiritual warfare of some sort. However, I could not pinpoint my enemy. I cursed the day I signed Scorpion Legal membership.

I failed to stomach that I had been fired without due process, without expecting it and without honour even. Puzzled and dejected, I would hear my veins and my heart drumming into my lifeless future. Just when I thought I had it all figured out, once again my life was on life support, I was driving on a flat tyre. I wasn't sure if I was coming or going; my life was a catalogue of disaster.

What was I to do? Go back home and admit failure? Would the streets honour a man without means, without a spear, and without a catch? The puzzle of dejection winded on and my thoughts coiled together.

Home always had a sour calling for an unemployed man. Firstly, one gets disrespected by the community at large and your wife begins to find you useless beyond the bedroom and that is humiliation heaping upon humiliation. An unemployed man has a huge appetite both above and below the belt, hence a cause for frustration in many homes.

I decided not to tell my wife about what had befallen me. I was marketing for jobs left, right and centre, but nothing came up. A month passed and nothing came up. My groceries dwindled, I was drowning on my own, and no one could throw me a life jacket. I had no one to call my own in South Africa. Letters of grocery list began to arrive from my wife and children. I had no escape. I grew tired of holding it together and eventually broke the news to my wife. I knew my wife was very business minded, she would conceive a plan to keep our children in school. 'The secret to life is to marry a woman with brains. A woman who can survive and keep the family together even in your absence'. Those were the words Basekulu told us as boys growing up.

At least in flesh I was alive, although my dreams were withering and my manhood cast down. Cast down, not by a fellow son of the soil, but triumphed upon by the feet of a stranger.

At that point, I felt that instead of wallowing in despair, perhaps I could cast my lot in the courts of law. I had to make use of the Scorpion cover that I had been paying for, for several months. When I visited their offices, the law seemed to be on my side. It was an unfair dismissal, no doubt. I was asked if I had ever signed any employment contract. I had not. Whether I had, or had not, I got the impression that my dismissal was unfair and ought to be taken up to the labour court.

After three fruitless court sessions, I felt like I was running a marathon with no finish line in sight. I ran out of taxi fare to and from the court cases. I also thought that, even if I won the case, how was I to work for the Bothas without bad blood between us? They would definitely make my life a living hell. It was like killing a cow you would want to milk. I stopped attending the court cases and never answered calls from Scorpion lawyers.

I made peace with my situation; after all, life does not take a break on anyone. Winter was approaching and I thought of the bale factory I had seen at the Randburg Industrial area. I decided to bait with my little savings by buying 10kgs worth of jackets. The jackets were a second hand lot from bales imported overseas. They were not sold in singles, but weighed in kilogrammes. I bought them with the intention of reselling them to people in my community, and scan the market to see the feasibility of the business for future purposes.

The jackets were creased from being compressed in bales and some of them had stains yet others needed a sewing touch up to make them appealing for resale. As soon as I got home, I washed them, ironed them and made sure to sew those that needed to be sewn and packed them nicely in a bag. I went around selling them at a reasonably cheap price. Within one hour, they were all sold. I had nailed a jackpot. I learnt to never undermine the buying power of people residing in informal settlements.

I started selling those jackets weekly until almost every household in Kya Sands informal settlement bought one. Kya Sands was one neighbourhood where the rich and the poor were divided by a road. On the other side of the road, Kya Sands was an affluent suburb whose inhabitants were predominantly Abelungu living in houses with big yards, with green lawns and trees. On the other side of the road were shacks made of corrugated zinc with no proper ablution and a lifeless vegetation. Black unemployed and blue-collar citizens lived in the latter.

My business targeted the side of the road where citizens were friendly, where I did not have to use an intercom to announce my arrival. Carrying a bag itself was significant enough that I was selling something. A side of the road where no one could imagine or ask me if I had stolen the goods. A side of the road where even those without money had the decency to fit the jackets and assured that they would support the business next time.

When I exhausted my target shack market, I moved to the next shack community. Others told me to come on their pay dates, which I did. Business was booming. At the same time, I often felt that the job of carrying jackets and selling door to door was not manly. It was a woman's job to knock door to door. Women have a nice way of talking their way and enhancing customers to buy. I was just a poor man compelled by my situation. Life in Johannesburg somehow robbed a man of his manhood.

As soon as winter passed, the jacket business slowed. It began to dawn that this was a seasonal business and I could not entirely depend on it. I went back to square one; I had to conceive another plan, probably back home.

Back home, the Zimbabwean economy steeped and eventually worsened. A few years ago, around the year 1997, all war veterans were called in the country and we were compensated with an amount of $50 000 which was deposited into our accounts after series of interviews, serious paperwork and verification of our details. At the time, when the Zimbabwean dollar had value, the amount could buy at least two houses in cash in the suburbs. Instead of investing in property as most of my counterparts did, I decided to save $35 000 in my bank investment account for the university education of my children. With that kind of investment, I imagined myself living my best life and sending my children to the best universities, possibly out of the country about 10 years later.

In the year 2000, the Zimbabwean government made a referendum on the country's constitution to acquire land from White farmers without compensation. The land reform was a fast track and resulted in the US and Britain imposing sanctions on Zimbabwe. The country's economy began to dwindle. As a result of the economic meltdown, grocery store shelves became empty and the Zimbabwean dollar became useless until the country had to adopt the South African Rand, the Botswana Pula and US dollar around the year 2008. Most of the country's basic needs were imported from South Africa and the neighbouring Botswana. The country that was once the envy of Africa became shameful.

The $35 000 that I had saved in my investment account went down the drain with the country's economy and I never cashed out a single cent from my savings. My savings were thus, squirrelled away by circumstances beyond my control and not even the bank could redeem my money. The system failed me.

Life generally soured in the country; civilians would rob delivery trucks of bread, just to feed their families. What an extra-ordinary robbery! On the other side of the border in South Africa, people would do huge robberies like robbing cash in transit vehicles.

As the economic situation worsened in the country, unemployment statistics skyrocketed to more than 90%. Diaspora migration became the solution. People left the country in search for green pastures. It is said that after 2005, about four million Zimbabweans left the country voluntarily and involuntarily. Those who left involuntarily were forced by the brutal political circumstances. Of the four million Zimbabweans who left the country, three million are believed to be residing in South Africa.

Most Kalanga and Ndebele people from Zimbabwe had been in South Africa way before the dire economic conditions prevailed. They, like myself flew the country as a result of a faulty integration system after the war of liberation and Gukurahundi which left more than 30 000 people dead. Other than that, opportunities in the country were, to a larger extent unfairly distributed. The ethnic issue was never properly addressed; some ethnic groups triumphed over others in the country, while some had no choice but to pioneer diaspora migration in the 1980s.

I decided to start a send-money-home business. I believed that I had a fairly large market for that business to prosper. Every household I knew in my village and beyond had at least an individual working in South Africa and supporting their relatives with remittances. I therefore facilitated my wife to sell three of our cows and a few goats for a business start. We fought over this decision until she finally agreed. She had always considered me as not sound when it came to business.

Our business operated like this: I would charge R20 for every R100 sent home. The sender's relatives would collect their cash from my wife back home. To supplement this business, my wife also started a *mashonisa* business with 30% interest every month. If one failed to pay in the following month, she would also calculate interest from the intended interest. As a result, a person could borrow R100 in January, but spend the rest of the year paying the interest that accumulates over the months. If unpaid, by the end of the year, one would be owing more than R2000 when they initially borrowed R100. Community members were generally seduced by such an easy credit and the business blossomed.

I was sceptical about this mashonisa business, I thought it would land us in trouble when people failed to pay up. Lo and behold, the woman I married did not play games when it came to money. When her clients failed to pay up, she would go to their households and grab anything worth the amount owed. Some of the goods she seized stretched from wheelbarrows, scotch carts, ox drawn ploughs and bicycles. She would sell them after about two months if the owners did not redeem them timeously. As a result of that reputation, all her clients negotiated their paying terms upfront.

The kind of business we were in did not require me to reside in South Africa full time. I resented the idea of living in a shack when I had a proper home back home. I decided to stay home and only came back towards month-end to collect monies. At the end, my clients had to deposit money in my bank account and send proof of payment. I would cash out that money whenever I went back to South Africa.

Part of the reason why I decided to retire from the Johannesburg life was that I wanted to have a bond with my children. I felt I had deprived myself of watching them grow. When I was still employed, I would only see them for a minimum of two weeks in April, August and December and that was not a healthy relationship a father should have with his children. The long-distance marriage relationship with my wife was also not healthy. We deprived each other of our conjugal rights.

I would here and there get 'some' from willing givers out there when I couldn't bear the intensity of my salts. It was not easy staying away from my wife for more than three months. I wondered how my wife survived the hunger. Women are taught by the society and their Christian religion to bear their cross in solitude and avoid embarrassing themselves, their husbands and their families. Perhaps they are also strong enough to resist the temptations.

One thing I learnt in the journey of life with *omakhwapheni* (side women) is that, what begins as just a once off act could easily escalate to something. These women had a way of reincarnating back and attaching themselves to your life whether you like it or not. Omakhwaphen*i* also exaggerated their submission and overdid things to beat your wife and win your heart. Even between the sheets, they would go an extra mile, forcing you not to erase their image from your memory. They could even wash your feet and call you by surname or clan name to feed your ego, while your wife calls you by your children's name. They put a lot of effort even in serving meals. A mere plate of stiff pap would be decorated to resemble a plate served at an Italian restaurant.

* * *

The thought of journeying home was horrific sometimes, we called home Kuvukiland. Kuvukiland was originally an underdeveloped African Kingdom in Leon Schuster's comedy film "Mr Bones" which had an economic resemblance with our country Zimbabwe. The difference between the two countries (Zimbabwe and South Africa) was not only economic, but also geographic. Crossing the Limpopo, a river bordering South Africa and Zimbabwe at the Beit Bridge border post was always a dawn of reality. The Zimbabwean side was always lifeless; it looked like a cursed land. The sun would fry the panting earth dry, only stems of overgrazed yellow grass would be visible on the savannah lands. The earth also burnt like hot coals. The grass was literally greener on the South African side. I wonder if economic conditions had an effect on the geographical. The Limpopo River was like the biblical red sea, which separated Egypt from Canaan.

* * *

Upon arriving home, I was touched by how the village had aged my wife. The intense heat from the sun gave her an aged look and she wasn't as attractive as she was when we stayed together in Johannesburg. Other than the atmospheric conditions of being scorched by the sun in the village, the diet people had in the village was not really balanced. People ate stiff pap at least twice or thrice a day without supplementing it with any other meal. Relish was mainly in the form of dried vegetables and dried meat. In the village, there were no other ways of preservation to keep food fresh, drying was the only option and nutrients would be lost in the process. Despite her unappealing nature, I was destined to love her against all odds. It was I who couldn't afford a better life for her.

Although I had longed to stay with my children and watch them grow, after spending about two months with them, I started feeling extremely annoyed by their ingratitude sometimes. Those that started working, I felt they were not doing enough for our household, compared to how much their mother and I had suffered to raise them. In our culture, parents bore children not only for obvious reasons of family-hood, but to be taken care of at old age and for older siblings to take care of younger ones. Our African children should know that they are born with obligations and dodging them is not an option. We fought a lot whenever this matter arose, out of frustration, they would mention that they did not choose to be born, let alone being born into poverty. That provoked me to the bone.

After staying home full time, my relationship with my wife also stopped being rosy. She was very prickly in front of children, knowing well that our daughters would sympathise with her and take her side. Although we had moments of being at each other's throat, our ferocity towards each other was always short-lived. We forgave each other easily and quickly.

We had three daughters and one boy. Our first-born Thuli didn't care about anything. She was indifferent and seldom talked to anyone. She was only vocal when it came to teasing others or cracking jokes. Theresa the second born was bubbly and very energetic. She had taken after her mother when it came to business. She occasionally sold popcorn, sweets and snacks at school to generate her own pocket money.

The third-born, Muti was one of a kind, and quite difficult to understand. She had multiple personalities. She had a calm demeanour albeit unpredictable sometimes. She had a yo-yo like temper and seldom exploded when someone treaded on her corns. As a result, we all avoided crossing her path, especially in front of people. She could easily embarrass one publicly no matter the age.

Khumo was very witty and had gimmicks that drew the attention of elderly men. He was very stunted in growth just as I was at young age. He wore three sizes smaller than his age but he was mentally mature like an aged wine. He was however a cry-baby to his mother as he was the last born and the only boy. I personally had no time for his childish nonsense. I often ridiculed his mother for raising a boy child under petticoats.

As the family's financial situation bettered, we sent Khumo to a boarding school when he was in Grade 4, as a result, he became untouchable and slippery from children his age. He saw himself as different from other children in the village. He had succumbed to the Englishness of the boarding school and would overly speak English even when it was not necessary. He preferred a highly imagistic English vocabulary that would silence other children in the village.

One of his greatest weaknesses was that he was incapable of thinking about tomorrow. Whenever one gave him money during the holidays, he would buy sweets and not think about the dry days of boarding school.

Other than the differences amongst ourselves as a family, we enjoyed teasing one another and giving people nick names such that we would gossip about them even in their presence. I remember one old man in the village who was suspected to be involved in witchcraft and was said to possess a huge snake, we called him *Snekere*, a name derived from 'snake', but with a humorous face beat to it. In this way, no one outside our family would understand when we gossiped about people.

* * *

Business went well and the profits heightened. We managed to save and build a shop at the growth point to multiply our streams of income. Upon introspecting my life, I realised that I started putting my mind to usefulness the day I stopped looking for a job. That is when I began to live.

~The end~